HOMELESS
FREE AS A BIRD

Clive Ward

Copyright © 2018 Clive Ward/oneroofpublications.com

All rights reserved.

ISBN-10: 1720693781
ISBN-13: 978-1720693789

DEDICATION

This book is dedicated to all members of the Armed Forces,
past and present

By Clive Ward

The Unnamed Soldiers
Army Barmy
Bumpers & Bed Blocks
EndEx
You Wouldn't Belize It
The Goat Killer

Writing with E Ward

Half Day Closing
In Sympathy

ACKNOWLEDGMENTS

I'd like to thank my wife and family for their constant support. Big thanks go out to Lynn Lawson for her patience and understanding whilst editing the manuscript. I'd also like to thank James Cooper for the moving poem he wrote for the book.

CHAPTER 1

It was getting late. I didn't have a clue where I was going to sleep tonight. Walking down the road away from my former home earlier that day, I'd felt a sense of release. It was time to put the past behind me. February and freezing, I'd picked the wrong time of year to become another homeless statistic, but shit happens. I'd been in worse situations, sleeping rough, what's new. I'd spent fourteen years in the army, most of the time doing exactly that, no worries bring it on. The only difference this time, I didn't know when Endex was going to be.

My first priority was that I needed to have a dump, no problem if I was in the middle of a training area or on patrol in Afghanistan, but I could hardly take a dump in the middle of the supermarket car park, next to a trolley bay. It was nearly ten o'clock at night so I just had time to nip into the store and use their trap doors before they closed. I passed the in-house security officer, who was far too busy texting away on his mobile to notice me as I entered their bogs. Leaving the cubicle, I quickly washed my hands, avoiding eye contact with the cleaner, who had just entered on his rounds. I felt sorry for the guy, having to put up with the smell I'd left behind. Now it was time to find somewhere to get my head down. I was looking forward to crawling into my sleeping bag. It had been a long day. I was due to be evicted from the house I rented at 9 am. I could have hung around and given the bailiffs a hard time or maybe talked them into letting me stay for one more night, but what was the point. I didn't have any bargaining chips left; it was game over. I decided to get out early and I was gone well before they arrived. The only possessions I had were in my Bergen, a sleeping bag, a small pop up tent, a change of clothes, a few family pictures and a large packet of digestive biscuits. I didn't want to take anything else from that place. It was all bad memories to me, a life I wanted to forget. I was emotionally shattered.

It started to snow and the temperature was dropping. Great! I needed to find shelter of some description before it got too bad. Walking across the road, I spotted an old guy sitting in the large doorway of a sex shop. I could smell him from twenty feet away. He looked like he was sleeping, the third rough sleeper I'd seen tonight. He was half sitting up, with his head tilted against the darkened glass, several empty lager cans lay beside him. There was a space next to him. It was the only dry place I could see, as the snow was coming down heavier and turning to slush, so I headed straight for it.

'Room for one more mate?' I asked. He didn't move.
'Shit, this bloke isn't dead, is he?' I thought to myself. I nudged him gently with my foot.

'Oi buddy, is this seat taken?' I said in a loud voice, almost shouting. When I say seat, I mean an abandoned breezeblock, which was next to him in the doorway.

Then it spoke. 'It's taken' he said in a slurred voice. He then proceeded to finish off a can of lager that he'd been hiding.

He was wearing a proper winter overcoat with big pockets, it wouldn't surprise me if he had half a dozen cans of lager hidden in there. I was expecting him to pull out a half-eaten kebab any second. He also wore cut off woolly gloves and a large woolly hat that covered his ears. It reminded me of one of those old, fashioned tea cosies, or one of those Cossack fur hats.

Just then, a dog appeared from nowhere. Looking like a drowned rat, it took up residence exactly where I was going to park my rear end. It was a mixed breed, a cross between a Jack Russell and a sausage dog. The dog looked up at me with sheepish eyes, and then looked at his owner, then back at me again. Its face had, 'you're not going to kick me out of this space, are you?' written all over it. The sad looking eyes made me feel guilty for asking about the space, even though there was plenty of room.

'Your dog, what's his name?' I asked.

He still didn't move, but I got an answer. 'He hasn't got a name.'

'Come on, he's got to have a name.' I got down on one knee to stroke the dog and fed him half the digestive biscuit I'd been eating. The dog with no name gladly tucked in.

'Well, are you going to let me in, there's more than

enough room in here for all three of us,' I asked.

The old man reluctantly shuffled over, sat up, and opened another can of lager.

'Thanks very much,' I said. I was glad to have found a dry spot to settle in for the night.

He didn't answer. I rearranged my sleeping area by refitting the cardboard carpet tiles and moving the discarded lager cans. I sat down, thankful that the dog with no name was between us. So, there I was sitting in a sex shop doorway, on a freezing cold night, with a scabby dog and a smelly old man with a belly full of 'lager, which I supposed was his central heating. I hope I don't go that far down hill, a rocket-fuelled existence wasn't for me. This was going to be a temporary fix. This guy wasn't like the other rough sleepers, he reminded me of the tramps my old man used to tell me about when he was a kid in the seventies. He looked like he'd been on the streets for years. I wondered if this guy I'd just met had a tramp name. My dad had told me there were always a couple of older gentlemen and ladies of the road knocking about back then. Their favourite spot was the church wall at the bottom of his street. They'd always frequent that spot, drinking cider or whatever they could get their hands on, hoping to scrounge a few pennies from unwilling commuters walking from the railway station.

My dad said the two tramps he remembered most of all were called Bokker and Winnie. He remembered teasing them and calling them names. He would shout 'you dirty old bastards, get a wash,' to try and get a reaction from them. He told me, one lunch break from school, Bokker charged at him and his friends with a surprising vigour. He chased them around the streets with a broom handle, which had a big knife fastened on the end of it! Shouting '*GERONIMOOOOOOO*,' he caught my dad's mate Simon and leathered him. They never reported it, as back then, being chased was all part of the fun. They were always trying to provoke the tramps from across the street. My dad said it didn't take long before the tramps started throwing their empty bottles at him and his friends and there were no plastic bottles in those days. But, it was my dad and his friends who ended up with egg on their faces one afternoon. Someone had grassed them up. The police turned up and made my Dad and his mates go home to pick up a dustpan and brush and then sweep up all the broken glass. The tramps just sat there and laughed along with the coppers, who knew once my dad and his friends got home, they'd get a good thrashing from their mum or dad. Back then people treated them with a bit more respect, even though they were dossers. **After that incident, Bokker used to call at my dad's house, and his mum would always feed the tramp, but only in the garden.** As my dad got older, he used to sit and listen to Bokker and his stories of the open road. **Once my dad and his friends formed a bond with the tramp,** they used to get him to buy fags and booze for them.

I was going to try and spark up a conversation with my new friend, but he was well gone, and snoring his head off. I think he'd had his quota, bless him. With the sound of the church bells striking midnight in the distance, and my new friend and his dog sound asleep, I took my sleeping bag out of my Bergen and joined them. There was no room to jump inside, so I just covered it over me. Apart from waking up during the night to find the sleeping bag covering all three of us, I slept well, under the circumstances. I could sleep anywhere. It was a military thing, something you never lose.

CHAPTER 2

Still half asleep, I felt a slight kick in the ribs. I was in that zone, where you've just woken up, wondering where I was. What the hell was that, what's happening? Surely, it's not my stag, where's my rifle? I thought I was back on sentry duty in the army. Then it suddenly dawned on me where I was. The owner of the sex shop had woken me up. He stood over me smoking a cigarette and he didn't look happy. The old man and his dog had moved on. The previous day must have been more tiring than I realised, as I hadn't heard them leave.

'Come on you, move it. I've got a business to run. And take your crap with you. I shouldn't have to put up with this every bloody morning, you lot are a pain in the arse.'

Apologising, I jumped up, grabbed my stuff and started to walk away.

'Haven't you forgotten something?' the sex shop owner called out.

I stopped. I walked back towards him and he handed me a wallet. I don't know why I didn't tell him it wasn't mine. I just took it. It might be full of money and that would definitely come in handy. Then I thought it might belong to that old tramp and it could be all he had left of his former life.

'Cheers pal, thanks for your honesty,' I said.

'You'll need that to buy your drugs with,' he said sarcastically. 'Just don't let me catch you sleeping in my doorway again. People like you bring the neighbourhood down.'

A bit ironic coming from a porn peddler I thought. I ignored his comment about buying drugs, even though it annoyed me.

'I said I was sorry ok,' I said, as I turned to walk away.

It was what he said next that lit the touch paper.

'And get a job, you, scruffy cunt.'

That was it. The red mist had set in. I walked back towards him, grabbed him by his collar and pushed him against the wall. I saw his eyes widen with shock and fear. He should be afraid; I was going to make him regret opening his mouth.

'What did you say? Get a job? You cheeky cunt!' Listen, I had a job, a good job. Any thick cunt can sell dildos and blow-up dolls, you fucking prick.'

'Alright mate, calm down, I apologise, let me go, you're hurting me.' he said with a trembling voice.

I was about to lay into him. I'd drawn my arm back, ready for the first punch, when a policeman who had been passing in his patrol car dragged me away from him.

'What's all this about?' the policeman asked.

I said nothing; I just stood glaring at the sex shop owner, trying to bring my anger under control.

'It's him officer, all I said was get out of my shop doorway and he hit me.'

'Hit you. If I had hit you pal you'd have known about it,' I retorted.

'Ok, that's enough. Do you want to make a complaint, sir?' The policeman asked the shop owner.

'No, it's ok. It's a good job you came along when you did, as God knows what could have happened. He's crazy and what's the betting he's got dirty needles on him. I pay my council tax. I don't have to put up with this officer.'

The policeman turned to me. I wondered if he was going to arrest me, regardless of what the shop owner wanted.

'What are you doing sleeping in doorways anyway? You don't look homeless, are you homeless?' he asked.

I didn't say anything; I just stood there, playing the naughty schoolboy. I knew if I opened my mouth, I'd probably say the wrong thing.

'If you are homeless, there's no shame in seeking help. There are plenty of charities who rescue people from the streets,' he added.

'I don't need any help, I can rescue myself,' I replied.

'Right then, off you go, move along,' he said.

I had the feeling the policeman was relieved not to be bogged down with an enormous amount of paperwork this early in the morning. He was either at the beginning of his shift or at the end. And as far as the porn peddler was concerned, I know why he didn't want to complain. 'Sex shop owner assaulted outside his shop,' is probably what the local newspaper headline would read, publicity he could do without, I should imagine. I'll just make sure that when I pass his doorway again in the dark hours, I'll leave him a nice present, an unwanted mister whippy.

I can't believe it, my first night as a homeless person and I'm already getting into shadow boxing like a tramp, and I hadn't even had a drink. I couldn't help it. I had one of those faces, my ex-army buddies used to say. It wasn't the first time I'd got myself into scuffles like that and it won't be the last. Back when I was in the army, getting into fights was a regular occurrence, either with another unit or the local civvies. I carried on walking and walking, just to keep warm. I didn't know where I was going, but at least it had stopped snowing.

After warming myself up, I sat down on a bench; soon I was deep in thought. Was this really what I wanted? I could easily walk a mile up the road to one of my friends' houses, if I wanted to, and they'd help me out, I know they would, or even jump on a bus to my parents house, they'd take me in. What was stopping me? No, I had to get those thoughts out of my head. I needed to sort this problem out myself. I didn't want the easy option. For now, all I needed was a mission, something to take my mind off my predicament. I'd made up my mind that it was now time for operation wallet. I needed to give this guy his wallet back, that's if it is his wallet of course. That was my mission.

But first, breakfast. I had a few pounds left on me. I could see the McDonald's sign in the distance and my belly was talking. I'd kill for a sausage and egg McMuffin! Maybe kill was the wrong word to use after what had just happened. Before I entered, I sat outside and checked out the contents of the wallet. Inside I found a ten-pound note, a bankcard, an old military ID card and a picture of a girl who must have been around my age and was very pretty. Could it be his ex, or maybe his sister? I wondered how old the picture was. It could be anyone. On the back of the photo was a telephone number. I pulled out the ID card, Lance Corporal Thomas Rogers. Well, well, well... the old boy was a squaddie just like me. The difference being that Lance Corporal Rogers was a dinosaur of the finest order; he had a regimental number from the seventies. The Op Banner Brigade or later called 'one of Maggie's children'. He must be in his late fifties or older by my reckoning. Remembering his face, he looked about that age. Then I took a closer look at the ID photo. Yes, that was him alright. I wondered what unit he was in, it didn't say.

What's a poor guy doing wandering the streets at his age? He should be given help, not left to rot on our streets. This shouldn't happen; the guy served his country. I wonder how many there are out there like Thomas. He could be a father, a grandfather, with a proud family. He had fought for his country back in the day. I wondered how many ex-servicemen and women were living on the streets. There is money for every crackpot scheme you can think of except for our homeless. An Ethiopian girl band got five million. They spend millions getting the Royal Navy to pick up migrants off the North African coast and bring them here and house them. But one thing never changes; our homeless get ignored. They can't find enough money to look after our own. Especially our veterans, they deserve better.

I sat in McDonald's, munching on my sausage and egg McMuffin, wondering where he'd moved on to. I needed to find him. I know I could ring the number on the back of the photo, but that would be too easy and wouldn't be right. Maybe he's running from the girl, who knows? I could end up opening a right hornets' nest. No, I will do it the hard way and track him down. I walked around town for most of the day, checking all the doorways, shop entrances and benches, even skips, he could be anywhere. I asked everybody I passed, 'You haven't seen an old tramp with a dog, have you?' 'Mate there are old tramps with dogs everywhere,' was the popular answer. Most people I asked just blanked me, no one had seen him, and he'd just disappeared without a trace.

The next few nights were dry, but still very cold. I managed to find a place to put up my tent in the local park. The park was locked from 9 pm so no one bothered me. I managed to stay there for three nights, and then my luck ran out. A security guard doing his mobile rounds moved me on. The next night the weather took a turn for the worse, it snowed heavily and the temperature plummeted to minus three degrees. All I could think about was how the old boy was coping. I'd slept in all sorts of weather in the army, minus three was nothing, but that night the conditions beat me, I'd been a civvy for too long. I was cold, wet and hungry and running out of funds. So, I made the decision to approach one of the homeless charities. After contacting the Salvation Army, they arranged for me to spend the night in a local hostel. You need a referral from an agency or an organisation like the Salvation Army to get into many hostels or night shelters. Some hostels run a waiting list. Luckily, they offered me a space to sleep.

The hostel took what bit of money I had left. Most hostels charge rent but the amount varies. You don't usually have to pay a deposit or rent up front, you can pay later, when they get you to claim housing benefit. But I told them my situation was temporary and I just wanted to stay for a few nights. I had somewhere else to stay after that, I said. So, I just had to pay a service charge for meals, heating and laundry, plus two days rent, which came to fifteen quid. I was learning fast and I was so happy to be out of the cold with a warm meal inside me. All hostels have their ground rules and this one was no different. You are asked to leave if you break the rules. The staff expected you to have a bath, while you are there and wear the clean clothes they give you, which have been donated to them by local charities. Most of the homeless people hated the idea of having a bath. And as far as the old tramps go, you'd be lucky if they have one bath a decade. I wished them luck with that one. And when it came to clothes, they were the only possessions they had, the poor fuckers. My clothes weren't that far gone yet, so they left me alone. They had strict rules on anti- social behaviour too. Most of the guests found it impossible to go more than an hour without shouting at the staff, especially the druggies. I asked the hostel staff if they knew of Thomas and his dog. After I described him, they knew of him all right. Tom, they called him, always coughing, they told me he had stayed a few times. Every time he stayed there he always caused trouble, so they had to bar him. But they said that was months ago.

After two days I left. I'd never seen anything like it before. There were people with mental issues and alcoholics, but most of the guests there were druggies, hooked on something called spice, it was so sad. I'd never been around drugs before and it was just horrendous. If I was ten years younger I might have seen the appeal of it to take those demons away because I was suffering. But no, drugs weren't going to solve my problems. There were dozens of charities

I could have gone to for help but this was my choice. I wanted to be on the streets, at least for now anyway.

CHAPTER 3

The weather had improved slightly so I spent the next couple of weeks sleeping where I could. Sitting in shop doorways or on benches, anywhere really, as long as it was dry. Sitting around all day watching the world go by wasn't too bad at first, then it started to get a bit boring. So, I spent a lot of time at local libraries, until I got asked to leave. It was probably due my aroma of urine and despair. You can only go so long without a good wash before people start to notice. I got money where I could. I hated begging, but I had to eat, I managed to beg enough money for a bag of chips most days. I even tried begging with a sign saying "veteran, please help." But my conscience got the better of me and I threw the sign away.

I still remember the passers-by who showed me kindness, like the woman who was shopping with her kid. When she saw me she sent her daughter back into the shop to buy me everything, a sandwich, drink, crisps and a dessert and then when she was halfway down the street she saw another homeless person and sent the child back into the shop to buy the same for them. Yes, there are some kind, generous people out there, and some people who look at you as if you are a piece of shit. I just politely smile and think to myself, 'you could be one payday away from being like me arsehole.' I didn't just live on chips. On other days I'd be in the supermarkets, looking out for the reduced priced food items, sometimes I'd get lucky, that's if others like me hadn't got there first. I hadn't resorted to looking in bins like some of them, yet. But I knew I was, capable of doing that, if I had to. Back in the army, stuck in camp over the weekend, with no money, late on a Saturday night, most squaddies would eat anything. It was a long time between tea and Sunday morning breakfast, half eaten pizzas and kebabs were the favourites, as, long as it was edible, it was food.

If I was going to survive out here, I had to get money another way. I had relatives and friends locally, who I knew would help me out if I asked them. But I was too proud; I didn't want them to see me like this. I couldn't face them. Not yet anyway. When I left the army, I handed over my ID card and kit and that was it. I was forgotten. And that's how it felt now. A few nights later, after a Baltic night, I was back in the hostel again. I wasn't coping very well. I signed all the forms for housing benefit and they let me stay. Talking to the staff and doing some serious thinking, I decided this life, as a homeless person was not for me. I'd had enough, what a miserable existence. I'd barely lasted a few weeks and I'd made the decision. 'I'm not a tramp get me out of here.' It was time to face the music, time for a stint of sofa surfing around my friends' houses, until I was back on my feet. For the first time in a while I felt positive.

This was going to be my last night of homelessness. Tomorrow it was go back to start, but there was no collecting two hundred quid. It was a pity I had to share it with the guy laying on the bed next to me. He was massive. He must have weighed about thirty stone. He was wearing grubby white trainers, that looked like they had had a row with his trousers, and an old grey coat, held together with a piece of the obligatory string. With his long black matted beard and dreads that looked like they were stuck together with glue, he looked a scary character. There was one more less than redeeming feature about him, the guy stunk; it must be a special aftershave they all seem to wear, an exclusive 'tramp only' brand. He was proper minging, but I was getting used to that by now, I'm sure I smelt just as bad. A lot of the smells in this place reminded me of being on exercise with the army. Such as the smell of gonk bags, or the smell of festering army dogs when you'd taken them off back at camp, after wearing them for a few days or weeks. Going weeks without a proper wash, I knew all about that, but this guy's smell reminded me of old camouflage nets that had been stored for months before the next exercise, and then bought out again to air, only to find a few dead rats entangled in it. Sad to think that the last words those rats ever heard were, "This is zero to all call signs, ENDEX."

That night, my last night, I couldn't sleep; someone was either farting or snoring. I just lay there awake thinking about how I was going to get back on my feet and what I was going to do with the rest of my life. The people running the hostel gave me some real good advice. There was lots of help out there, if I really wanted it. I wonder if they'd let me join back up again, surely at thirty-two I'd be too old. It was around one in the morning and I was just about to finally drift off to sleep when I heard a noise. I opened my eyes and my night vision clicked in. I saw the man mountain that was sleeping next to me, rummaging through my Bergen, the sneaky fucker. I just lay there and watched him, contemplating my next move. He found the wallet and proceeded to put it in his pocket.

'Oi, what do you think you're doing? You thieving bastard.' I made him jump.

'Are you talking to me, sonny?' he replied.

'Yes, put it back.'

'Put what back?' he asked, feigning a look of innocence.

I didn't waste any time, there was one thing I couldn't abide and that was a thief. I jumped on him and we started to wrestle on the floor. I just wanted the wallet back. At one stage he had me in a headlock. I had to submit. It wasn't that he was hurting me, it was the smell coming from his armpits. I wasn't sure if I was going to throw up or pass out, the smell was that strong. It was disgusting.

'Ok, ok, you win, let go,' I replied, gasping.

Like a twat, he let go. After both of us had taken a few blows from each other, this time it was me who had him in a headlock. I kept punching and punching him in the head. It had no effect. This guy was as strong as an ox and smelt like one too. It was a proper bum fight. I started to tire, he was starting to get the better of me and by this time the staff had been alerted. I had just managed to get the wallet back, when they intervened and managed to pull him off me. They didn't tell us, but they had already called the police and they were on their way. The guy was still trying to attack me when they arrived.

'Come on Yogi, calm down,' said one of the coppers. They obviously knew him; he must have previous. Yogi was having none of it; he was ready to take the world on.

It was only when they pointed their Tasers at him, he gave up. He put his hands up and laid face down on the ground. It seemed like he'd had a taste of the

Taser before. We were both arrested and taken to the local police station. Arriving at the station, Yogi and I were both booked in by the staff in the custody suite.

'Name?' the custody sergeant asked.
'Jones.'
'Full name?'
'Andy Jones.'
'Address?'
'Anywhere.'
'No fixed abode then?'

To be honest, the coppers were very good to me. I hadn't been drinking, unlike the guy I'd been fighting with. Who was by now shadow boxing, singing a mangled version of Delilah by Tom Jones. I was right; Yogi was a regular. He was soon escorted to one of the cells.

'Come on Yogi, let's get you to your cell, number five, home sweet home,' the escorting officer said.

Fuck me, he had his own personal cell. I was to follow. I wasn't complaining though, I was happy to be one of their detainees for the night, excited at the prospect of spending the night on a rubber mattress in complete safety. Instead of a cold, sex shop doorway, bus shelter, or worse. After a quick brew, which they so kindly supplied me with, it wasn't long before I was flat on my back in my nice warm cell. With the faint sound of Yogi singing, his very own version of a Sinatra classic, eventually the singing subsided, and I was soon knocking out the zeds.

CHAPTER 4

The next morning, I woke up to the sound of cell doors opening and closing, and someone coughing their lungs up. I then remembered what had happened the night before and wondered what the consequences would be. I was only defending myself; well actually that's wrong, I started it.

Last night I had steam coming from my socks when I placed them on the radiator, now they were dry, it sort of gave the cell a homely smell. From the look on his face, I could tell the PC that opened my cell door didn't think that.

'Jesus H Christ, it bloody stinks in here,' he said, screwing his nose up.

'I'm sorry about that,' I replied, feeling slightly embarrassed.

'It's ok, I've smelt worse, I can assure you. Here's your breakfast.'

Breakfast wasn't much to shout about, but there were no complaints from me. At least it stopped my stomach rumbling from hunger. With my new shiny black eye and cut lip, I was starting to look like a tramp.

At eight o'clock I was back in front of the desk sergeant being cautioned and lectured on my behaviour. I was then given some advice and a bundle of help leaflets.

'You're a lucky lad. I'm releasing you without charge. If I find you in here again, you'll be up in front of the magistrates. Go and sort yourself out.'

I took in everything he said.

'Yes Sergeant.'

Bloody hell, it felt like I was back in the army, how many times have I said that!

He then gave me back my belongings. Luckily, they didn't discover the wallet hidden in the lining of my Bergen. If they had done, I'm sure there would have been questions asked. Nor could I have told them that the reason I was fighting him was to get the wallet back. This had been one big eye opener for me. Yet another reason I didn't want to be on the streets. It was then, out of the corner of my eye that I spotted Tom, the old tramp I'd been looking for, I was sure it was him. He'd only been in the next cell to me all night!

'Tom, where have you been? I've been looking everywhere for you,' I called out.

Tom looked confused, I could understand that, the last time he saw me he was out of his face on lager. He was probably wondering how I knew his name.

'Yes, it was like the tramps ball in here last night. Do you two know each other?' the desk sergeant asked.

'No,' said Tom sternly.

'Yes, you do,' I said.

'Well, do me a favour Tom, will you take lover boy and get out of my station.'

We both walked outside and stood on the police station steps. It was good to breathe in the fresh air, even though it was another freezing cold day. I bet the police were just as glad. Tom was dressed in that large overcoat, the very same one he was wearing a few weeks ago, when I first met him. And his oversized tea cosy hat and cut off gloves. With his baggy, piss stained trousers; he looked like your typical gentleman of the road, a proper throwback to the old days, when tramps were tramps.

'How the fuck do you know my name, who are you?' he asked.

'It was on your ID card corporal,' I said, trying to be witty. I took his wallet out of my Bergen and gave it to him.

'That's yours, isn't it?'

The reaction I got surprised me, he just sat down on the police station steps and burst into tears.

'Steady on old man, what is it, are you ok?'

'Where did you find it?'

'We spent the night together in the sex shop doorway, you must have dropped it when you left.'

'I can't remember that, I don't even know what day it is half the time.' He then started to cough, the same cough I'd heard in the cells last night and this morning.

'It's Friday,' I told him, feeling sorry for him.

'Thanks mate, you don't know how much that wallet means to me, let me buy you a cuppa,' he said, looking down at his left wrist at his non-existent watch, which I found bizarre. 'Come on, it's nearly half past eight, she'll be opening up about now.'

We started to walk up the street. I wondered who 'she' was.

'Sorry, what did you say your name was?' he asked.

'Andy, but who's going to serve us, we look like tramps,' I replied.

'Look like tramps! We are fucking tramps,' he said.

We both laughed. I'd broken the ice. We had something in common; we both had a sense of humour.

'Come on, follow me,' he said

It was obvious Tom was well known because he was greeted with 'good morning Tom' by most of the shopkeepers. I had promised myself, whilst in the cell, that I'd get myself sorted as soon as I got released. But that could wait. After looking for this guy for a few weeks, the least I could do was take him up on his offer of a free cuppa, plus I was intrigued. I wanted to find out more about **Thomas Rogers**. We arrived at a small café called Angie's Place, about four hundred yards from the police station. Before we entered, he told me the café was a special place and I wasn't to tell anyone else about it, which I thought was odd.

'Morning Tom, Oh, you've bought a friend' said a middle-aged, glamorous looking woman. She had that Barbara Windsor look about her. She was smartly dressed, as though she was about to meet the queen. The café was very clean, tidy and tastefully set out. It had a Mediterranean theme about it. I introduced myself and we sat down.

'Right, what can I get you gentlemen?' she asked.

'Two teas please Angie,' Tom replied.

'Can I use your toilet please?' I said.

'Of course you can dear, it's first on the right.'

Angie didn't properly open her doors to the public until 9am, before then, she opened her doors to the great unwashed. It was a thing she had done every Friday for years, Tom had told me. I could tell Tom was one of her favourites. I arrived back and sat down.

'What's your name son,' Tom asked.

'Andy, Andy Jones... I thought I told you.'

'And I told you I have a problem remembering things. Eh, you're not a Taffy are you?'

'Nah...what's wrong with Taffy's anyway?'

'Nothing, it's just I a guy I met a few years back, he was a Taffy. The guy would never shut up about rugby, and he still owes me five quid.'

'Why didn't he give it you back?'

'He said that when I lent it him a few years back, the old five pound notes were in circulation, now they are not legal tender. So, he says he doesn't owe me anything. I haven't seen him for a while. I met him when I was on the streets in London, before I moved up here. So, what's your story Andy?' Tom said, stirring his tea.

'I haven't got a story really.'

'Did you hear that Angie? He says he hasn't got a story.'

Angie laughed as she carried on making sandwiches behind the counter.

'Everyone's got a story, why have you chosen the streets? What's your addiction, is it drugs or alcohol,

PTSD, bereavement maybe?' he probed.

'None of them, I'm out on the streets by choice,' I replied.

'The first step for any addict is to recognise that they have a problem. Don't worry, this is not an interrogation, you're not back in the military. You're a veteran aren't you? What mob was you in?'

'Infantry, the Mercian Regiment, how did you know I was a vet?' I asked. Surprised at how astute he was.

'I can recognise a veteran anywhere. There are enough of them on the streets.'

'Takes one to know one,' I said.

'If you say so, come on, tell the truth, you like a drink, don't you?' he replied.

'No, not really, occasionally I might have the odd lager or beer.'

'It's drugs then.'

'Not a chance.'

'PTSD?'

'Stop interrogating the poor lad, Tom,' Angie said.

'No, I just found myself out on the streets. It's a long story mate,' I answered, not willing to talk about my past.

'It's no place for a young man like you, especially this time of year,' Tom replied.

'Not for long, this is my last day, so you needn't worry about me. I'll be alright.'

'Really, have you just decided that?' Tom asked.

'Being homeless is not for me. I just can't see a future in it.'

We both laughed. I definitely had the same sense of humour as him. Then he started to cough.

'And anyway, what makes you so special? You shouldn't be on the streets either, judging by the sound of that cough. That doesn't sound good mate, you need to see a doctor and get it sorted.'

'I haven't got a doctor and anyway, the cough comes with the territory, we call it the street cough. A couple of cans will cure it. I've been on the streets a long time Andy. I know how to look after myself, I'll have you know.'

Tom obviously felt it was time to change the subject and began asking me about my stint in the cells.

'You didn't tell me why you ended up in the cells for the night,' he said.

'I got in a fight with a guy at one of the hostels, they called him Yogi.'

Tom started to laugh. 'Yogi, fat Yogi is harmless, as long as you don't upset him. You upset him, didn't you?'

'The bastard tried to steal your wallet while I was sleeping, if it wasn't for his smell waking me, he would have been away with it.' I shuddered as I recalled the overpowering smell of his body.

'I've come across Yogi a few times. He's a veteran, ex-Navy stoker I think. He's one of those who shouldn't be on the streets. He should have been sent to the basket weaving wards years ago. In the old days, there was a place for people like Yogi. He would have been placed in an asylum and been well looked after, if the government hadn't closed them all down. Sadly, I've met a lot of people like Yogi out here. They all should be in care.'

'Do you know what happened to Yogi? Why is he on the streets?' I asked.

'Nobody knows. He's a lot better than he was. I remember when I first met him in a hostel a few years back. He was just sitting there, laughing hysterically. I mean, it was one of those psychotic crazy laughs. Another time I caught him arguing with himself. Then he started slapping himself. Eventually we asked him what his problem was, and he just rattled off a story about how the Navy was feeding him special drugs, and he had to check in with them every twenty minutes, or else they'd trigger an explosion in his head. I think he's over all that now. Yogi is perfectly reasonable to talk to, until he's had his can of lager, at which point he will start singing along at the top of his lungs, thoroughly pissing off everyone who is around him. Years ago, it didn't matter where he was. Usually it would be in one of the pubs in town. We used to kid him on, that his voice sounded just like the King's. Anyone walking into the bar would say things like, 'who's put an Elvis record on, or 'not another Elvis record,' when in reality, his voice was shocking. It was all good fun; until one day some bright spark, that was probably having a Victor Mildew moment, told Yogi it was because of his shit singing that the pub was empty. He told him everyone was pissed off with him and hated his singing. Someone else said, 'yeah, we all do, now fuck off!'

Tom chuckled to himself before continuing.

'An upset Yogi disappeared out of the pub and came back twenty minutes later, plus one fence post that he'd pulled out of somebody's garden. He then proceeded to wreck the pub, along with three punters, who all ended up in hospital. **I think he's still barred from every pub in a ten-mile radius.** He got sent down for six months, but I heard he got an early release. The prison staff had had enough of his singing, I think it was jail house rock that did it for him.'

'Poor bloke,' I said.

To be honest though, I was glad of the night on a

rubber mattress, and the breakfast wasn't bad either, so he did me a favour, and I wouldn't have met up with Tom again. I suppose everything happens for a reason.

'You want to think yourself lucky, that's one of the only custody units left that still gives you a hot breakfast. There's no respect for gentlemen of the road anymore, in most other police stations, all you'll get is a poxy cereal bar.' Tom shook his head in disgust.

I smiled at his reply; it was obvious he was a frequent visitor to the police stations in the city. I wondered what he had done the previous day to warrant a night in the cells.

'What about you, how come you were in the cells?' I asked.

'It was kicking out time. I'd had a few and I was starving, so I thought I'd pinball my way over to the kebab shop for a discarded freebie. I sat on the bench hoping I'd get lucky, waiting for a free meal to end up in the bin. The customers always chuck them away at that place; he sells shit kebabs. Suddenly I looked around and fuck me it was like zombie dawn of the dead. I had competition. The local skip rats from the industrial estate were on the hunt for a midnight snack too. It's amazing to see what happens, when nearly a whole kebab is thrown in the bin. Result...utter fucking chaos! The dirty skip rats tried to beat me to it. It does prove one thing, it confirms they are able to focus and concentrate on something more than their next fix of spice. Anyway, It ended up Tom one, skip rats, nil; I won and the kebab was mine. Before I knew it, the owner of the kebab shop came running out and started giving me the verbal, saying I was putting off his customers. Of course I was putting the customers off; that was the fucking idea. It was the only way I knew of stopping them from getting Delhi belly. They didn't know it, but I was doing them a favour. After a few minutes of him pushing me around I'd had enough, so I threw what was left of the kebab at him. Oh yeah, followed by a nearby wheelie bin through his shop window. Before I knew it, the old bill arrived and I was banged up. I can't remember the rest.'

Again, Tom looked at his non- existent, watch. 'That's why I'm at the magistrates at one o'clock. In the old days when you got nicked for Breach of the Peace they threw you in the slammer overnight. As long as you didn't kick off they would release you in the morning with no further action taken, not nowadays. I wouldn't mind, but the kebab was minging.'

'Of course, it was minging, you'd taken it out of the bin,' I said.

'No, it didn't have any mint sauce on it,' he replied.

We both laughed.

'By the way, where's your dog?' I asked. 'You had a dog the other night, unless that was just a stray.'

'Oh, he's on death row, unless I pick him up from the RSPCA before four o'clock. They won't keep them forever,' he answered.

'I bet he's been having a whale of a time, living it up with all his doggy friends no doubt,' Angie said.

'So how come you ended up on the streets Tom?' I asked.

'I choose to be on the streets. I like it.'

'You like it, why?'

'I don't know. Maybe it's the total lack of responsibility that comes from being homeless I like. It's not as bad as you think you know, once you've learnt the art of tramp-ism.

'So, what did you do in the army then, Tom?'

'I don't want to talk about it.'

'Come on, why not, 2434, with a first four like that, my betting is you did Op Banner, or the Falklands didn't you?'

Tom got up sharply, knocking his chair over and looking down at me angrily. For a moment I thought he was going to take a swing at me.

'Like I said, I don't want to fucking talk about it,' he said.

'Tom, calm down mate, it's ok, no more questions, I promise,' I replied, hoping he'd sit back down.

It wasn't long before Angie was on the scene.

'Sit down Tom love, here's some biscuits' Angie said, trying to calm him down.

'Yes, sit down Tom. I meant no offence mate... fucking hell.' I couldn't understand why he was so angry. What had happened to him in the army, to make him not want to talk about it?

'And you can mind your P's and Q's young man' Angie admonished me.

'Sorry Angie,' I replied, feeling a little embarrassed.

We sat in silence for a while, and drank our tea and ate the biscuits, until Tom had calmed down. I felt guilty for upsetting him and vowed never to bring the subject up again. His time in the army was obviously a taboo subject.

'Come on gentlemen, it's time to move on now I'm afraid, I open up in ten minutes,' Angie said.

We got up to leave and she followed us to the door. I noticed she had a can of air freshener in her hand, I could understand why, we both must have smelt ripe.

Not the sort of smell you'd expect in an eating establishment.

'Thank you Angie, always good service as usual,' Tom said.

'That's ok; remember between eight and nine on a Friday my door is always open, as long as you behave yourself. Be careful out there boys and come again.'

As we walked away, I looked back and watched her nosily looking up and down the street. She then closed the door and turned the closed sign to open. I could imagine her spraying every nook and cranny with the air freshener.

'So, what now? I suppose you're off to find yourself again,' Tom said.

'Yep, I'm sure I'll be ok. In a few months time, you never know, if I'm walking downtown and see you, I might slip you a few quid,' I replied, glad he seemed to have got over his earlier bad mood.

'Good. I'll hold you to that,' he answered.

'And you, what will you do?' I asked.

'Oh, same old; I have a busy social life you know. Good luck young man. I hope you sort yourself out and thanks for giving me my wallet back.'

Tom then put out his hand and I shook it firmly as we said our goodbyes. Walking away in different directions, I felt a little sad at our parting. He was a sound bloke and funny at times. He was the first person I'd met on the streets that I sort of got on with. We both had the same sense of humour, the sort civvies wouldn't understand. Even though he practically bit my head off when I asked him what mob he was in, I still liked him. What must have happened for him to react like that? Poor fucker, what did the army do to him? Maybe he was Special Forces or something, most of them lot would never reveal what they did, not even to their own family. Oh well, I suppose I will never know.

CHAPTER 5

This was the start of a new chapter in my life. It was now time to get my act together; living on the street had been an experience I won't forget in a hurry. At least now, even though I'd only been on the street for a few weeks, I'll always see most homeless people in a different light. Before, like the majority of people, I tended to look the other way when I saw the homeless, whether they were veterans or not, for me it was avoiding eye contact at all costs, pretend they don't exist. Whether they are homeless, or tramps like Tom who choose to live rough on the streets, or are forced to be there due to addiction, for whatever reasons, I will always spare them a few quid from now on.

I walked for about two miles and arrived at my mate Jameo's house, he lived in a two bedroom terraced in a rough part of town. I knocked on the door. I didn't know what sort of reaction I'd get. I hadn't been in touch for a while. I'd, known Jameo since I was a kid. We were best mates before I joined up and reunited when I got out. His wife Kelly was my ex-wife Sally's best mate. They had two boys, Craig, who was three and Alex, who had just turned one. The door opened.

'Is that you Andy? Fucking hell mate, I didn't recognise you for a minute. What the hell happened to you? Come in mate, come in,' he said, opening the door wide.

I entered the living room and straight away made eye contact with his wife Kelly, who was standing in the kitchen doorway. She gave me a forced smile and then disappeared back into the kitchen, trying to make herself look busy. Little Craig was too busy playing with his toy cars to notice I was there.

'Sit down mate; Kelly put the kettle on love. It's Andy, he's come to see us,' he called out.

'I can see who it is. I'm in the middle of cleaning Alex's arse for fuck's sake, I can't do everything.'

'Never changes, does she? Always had a way with words, my Kelly,' Jameo said.

I could tell he was embarrassed by her reaction, the slight flush of pink in his cheeks was a dead give away.

'Listen, if this is a bad time?' I replied. I could tell Kelly was less than thrilled to have me sitting in her home.

'No, don't be stupid Andy; it's great seeing you again mate. I was starting to wonder where you'd disappeared to. Sorry about what happened to you and Sally, that was out of order that was.'

'Shit happens, eh Jameo, I'm moving on mate,' I answered, not wanting to discuss the breakdown of my marriage.

'So, where've you been? You just disappeared. Me and Kelly was just talking about you the other day. We were worried about you. How are you coping, where are you living?'

'Long story mate but I bet Sally's been in touch and given you her version of events.'

Just then, Kelly arrived in the living room holding the baby under one arm and my mug of weak tea in her other hand.

'No, we haven't heard from her have we Kelly?' Jameo said.

'Who Sally? Nope, not heard from her in weeks.' Kelly placed the mug of tea in front of me and left the room.

'Thanks Kelly,' I said, to her retreating back.

Jameo leaned over and whispered to me. 'She doesn't like Sally's new fella. So, carry on, you were saying Andy.'

'After what happened, I just wanted some time out. Listen Jameo, you couldn't do us a big favour could you? Any chance you could let me stay on your sofa for a few nights, until I've sorted myself out. I'm desperate mate.'

'Andy, I'd love to, but it's a small place, look, you couldn't swing a cat in here, you know what I'm saying. We're looking to move soon aren't we Kel,' he said, raising his voice, so she could hear him.

'Just the one night then Jameo, that's all I'm asking. I'll be out of your face tomorrow morning, first thing, I promise.' I took a sip of the tea and squirmed.

'What's up, no sugar?' Before I could take another mouthful, he took the cup off me. 'I'll nip in the kitchen and put some sugar in it for you.'

That was his excuse to consult the one who must be obeyed. I knew already what the answer would be. Jameo entered the kitchen and pushed the door to, leaving it slightly open. I could just about make out what they were saying.

'Not a fucking hope in hell Jameo, have you smelt

him, he bloody stinks. Look at him, he needs a bath and look at all those cuts and bruises on his face, he's obviously been in a fight or something. Do you seriously think I'd have him anywhere near my kids? No, Jameo and that's final.'

That was ironic, seeing as I was the kid's Godfather. How things change I thought. At one time they wouldn't have hesitated to offer me their sofa for the night.

'It's only for one night Kelly.' I could hear Jameo pleading my case.

'Not a chance, you better get your arse back in there and tell him, or I will.'

I saved him the embarrassment. Before he re-entered the front room, I was gone. I visited two more friends, one was on his holidays but the other one was in all right. I rang the doorbell several times but got no answer. As I walked away, I glanced through the window and saw him and his other half dodge behind the sofa. I think they must have already had the warning order from Kelly. What now? I wasn't doing very well. For a moment I considered my mum and dad, then thought no. Even though I loved them both to bits, I had my reasons.

I wandered back downtown. It was now nearly two in the afternoon. The only option left to me now was veteran's charities, but it was too late to start knocking on doors for professional help now, it was nearly the weekend. It looked like another few nights under the stars. The RBL would have to wait until Monday morning. Shit, I was becoming a proper homeless person now. I started to think about where I was going to doss down for the night. I could really do with a drink right now.

I walked through the town centre. Passing a well-known clothing store, I stopped and glanced at my reflection, it looked straight back at me. Fuck me, is that really me, I didn't like what I saw. I wouldn't get stick man at guard mount that was for sure. I looked terrible. With my black eye and cut lip, my general appearance was enough to put anyone off taking me in, especially in an environment where there were children. I couldn't blame Kelly for putting her foot down. What was I thinking?

What would I give for another night on that rubber mattress right now? I sat down on a nearby bench and watched the people head home to their nice warm houses after a hard day's work. To them, I was just another homeless person. I know, I'll make them notice me, why don't I throw a brick straight through this shop window, like Tom did with the wheelie bin last night. What was stopping me? At that moment, I didn't give a fuck what happened to me. I started to feel bad. It was certainly one of my lowest points. Was I starting to break down? Why me, where did it all go wrong? I'm not a bad person. Why me? **Homelessness was bad news. I felt like I was no longer a part of society. I'd fallen through the cracks and become nothing more than a statistic.** How many nights would a brick get me? What if I did something really bad, like find my ex-wife and strangle her? I could end up doing a long stretch in her majesty's prison for that one. At least in prison I'd be entitled to three meals a day, a shower every day, free healthcare and one of them miniature phones you shove up your arse. I had a mate who got sent down and he told me it was the closest thing to being back in the army. Most of the screws were ex forces anyway, who you could have good banter with, as long as you showed them respect. I wish I was in the US, I'd probably be looking at a full retirement plan. Life means life over there, unless you live in one of those death row states. If I was really clever, I could make out I was nuts, and live the rest of my days in luxury, wearing comfy slippers and get visits from Trevor McDonald and Louis Theroux. Fuck, I could really do with someone to talk to right now. I stayed on the bench for another few hours, then this random guy sat down next to me. He looked a little scary. He had piercing eyes and was shaking, rocking backwards and forwards. He was as wide as he was tall, his hands and neck were covered with tattoos. I wasn't worried; there were plenty of people around.

'Mind if I take a seat pal,' he said, in a Scottish accent.

'Be my guest. I haven't seen you around here before,' I replied.

'Nah, I've been away pal.'

'Anywhere nice?'

'Prison. I've just done a three year stretch.'

Alarm bells started to ring in my head. Was I safe sitting talking to this guy? What crime did he commit to get a three-year sentence?

'I was hoping not to be on the streets again, but you know how it is. I could've gone and stayed with friends, but they're all smack heads,' he continued speaking.

'So, you were on the street before you went to prison?' I asked.

'I've spent most of my life in prison, or on the streets. Before I got sent down this time I was doing methadone, heroin, crack, you name it. I was eight stone and nearly dead man; you know what I'm saying. But this time, I don't need that shit; I want to start again. You know what I'm saying?'

'I wish I could help you mate, but I'm homeless too.' He then put out his hand for me to shake.

'Don't you worry yourself man. I'm Jimmy by the way. What's your name?'

'Andy.'

'You haven't got a smoke, have you Andy?'

'No, sorry I don't smoke.'

'It's changed since I was last out here' said Jimmy. It's like that movie, 'Night of the Living Dead.' Half of them are just kids, that spice has got a lot to answer for. What about you, what's your story?'

'I've just had a hard time mate; my missus left me and I lost my house. I just wanted to get away. I don't want to be homeless forever but I need to make the best out of my situation. So, where are you staying tonight?' I asked.

'I'm sleeping in a bin room behind this building, it stinks, but it's away from the elements. The council has sorted me out with a bedsit. I move in Monday, all being well.'

'Good, I'm glad for you,' I replied and meant it. It was good to know someone was getting their life back on track. It gave me hope for my future.

With that, he got up to leave. 'Well, got to move on, nice to meet you pal and cheer up, things will get better, you'll see.'

'Good luck.' I said.

'You too, got to go pal. Remember, don't let the negative thoughts get to you, keep focusing on the positives.'

'I will.'

That little meeting bucked me up a bit. Come on Andy, I said to myself, you can do this. I headed for the park before it got dark, hoping the security officer wasn't around. I was starting to feel hungry. All I'd had to eat today was that shitty police station breakfast and a few of Angie's biscuits. Then I remembered, 'Biscuits!' I still had a few digestive biscuits left in my Bergen. While searching my backpack for the few broken biscuits I saw something that looked like a twenty pound note staring up at me from the open biscuit packet. I thought I was dreaming. What the hell! It was a twenty pound note. How did that get in there? Maybe Tom had put it in there. I thought for a minute, how did he manage to do that without me knowing? Then it came to me, in Angie's Place, while I was in the bog, the sneaky old fucker. I was so happy, wow, twenty quid! I sat on the park bench for a while looking at the twenty pound note, it had been a long time since I last saw one. I grabbed all my gear again and headed straight for the nearest shop. He must have known I'd be back out here tonight. That's if it was Tom of course.

Ten minutes later I was heading back to the park, the proud owner of an ounce pouch of tobacco and papers, a cheap disposable lighter, four cans of John Smith's, a packet of cheese and a loaf of bread. I felt like a king. The funny thing was, I'd packed in smoking four years ago and the last time I'd had a proper drink was back in the army. I remember a truly spectacular binge one night that saw me man-down and unable to move without throwing up until late the following afternoon. After that I swore I'd never drink again.

Sod the park I said to myself. I decided to head out of town and find some **woodland away from suburbia**. I was sick of seeing the same places and people. I had food and a bit of money. I was sharing it with nobody. So off I went, walking up the A6 towards Duffield, for a few days in the countryside. By the time I got there it was dark. I'd been walking for two hours. From the main road I headed up to the tree covered hills. I soon had my tent up, I was well away from the road and out of sight and it wasn't long before I got a bit of a fire going. I sat filling my face with bread and cheese, thinking about the day I'd just had with its ups and downs. With a full belly and a few beers down my neck, I'd soon forgotten about my earlier mini breakdown. I wouldn't have any problem sleeping tonight, plus there'd be nobody around to wake me, telling me to move on, like the security guard in the park. I sat outside the tent for a while, looking at the small spots of light from distant houses. It reminded me of being on exercise in the army, wishing I was in one of those nice warm houses, but tonight, I was happy to be free, to live my life as I wanted.

The next morning, I woke up feeling better, I'd overlaid. My built in clock was telling me it was around ten o'clock and time for breakfast. This time round the cheese and bread wasn't as appealing as it had been the night before. I thought I'd save that till later. I waited for the rain to stop, but it didn't. It rained all day, so I didn't go anywhere; I just lay in my sleeping bag thinking about my future, weighing up my options. I was already having second thoughts about getting help on Monday. Why? I didn't have a clue. Nobody was forcing me to live on the streets. My thoughts then drifted to Tom, how did he get on at the magistrates? Did he get the dog with no name back? I decided not to go looking for him this time. I'm sure our paths will cross again at some stage.

CHAPTER 6

A couple of days later I was back in town. I had a bit of Tom's money left, so I treated myself to a Big Mac, it was the first hot food I'd had since my breakfast at the police station.

A few more days went by and it was now Wednesday. I had to get some money from somewhere. I spent that day in the Market Place, trying to scrounge a few quid from passers-by, this time without success; most of them just took the piss. I just didn't have the skill levels that the other homeless people had. What could I do? I couldn't see me flogging the Big Issue and I was totally shit at playing a guitar, so busking was out. If I was going to survive out here I needed to learn, and quick.

I wandered around for most of the evening. It was now one in the morning on the coldest night of the year. I'm damp, chilled to the bone and starving. I've had enough. I need shelter from the freezing fog and sanctuary from the sinister characters prowling around. I'd slept in a doorway near the train station the night before but a gang of youngsters jumped me while I was asleep and threw a wooden pallet at me. If it had landed on my head I'd have been dead, the little shits. My best bet for sleep tonight looked to be a wooden crate and three cardboard boxes in the corner of a well-lit car park, just up the road from the police station. I was taking no chances.

I'd given up sleeping in my tent unless I was in a secure area, or out of town. A few young lads I could probably handle but I'd noticed there were a few unsavoury characters knocking about. I'd heard from a Big Issue seller, that last week in Nottingham some guy was attacked with a hammer while he was asleep in his tent. Curled up in his sleeping bag, unable to defend himself. Apparently, it was all about a feud over stealing someone's begging spot. I was just getting comfortable in my new-found spot. I'd zipped myself up in my sleeping bag, protected from the dirt and cold, when this large, booze-addled bloke in his forties sat down next to me. He opened a can of Strongbow and cackled with laughter as he accidentally spilt cider over me, soaking my sleeping bag. I didn't say anything, as I didn't want trouble, it wasn't worth it. Then I realised who it was. It was Jimmy, the Scottish guy I'd met last week in town, outside the clothing shop, the poor fucker. I guess he didn't get his flat then. I couldn't speak to him, he was shit faced, but I did make him a roll up. Minutes later, a bearded Romanian man appeared from nowhere. He stared down menacingly and barked: "You're on my bed. Fuck off Now!" I wasn't going to argue with him either; he was huge. I just grabbed my Bergen and trudged off into the cold night, in search of somewhere else to sleep. I was right to walk away that night. The story I read in a discarded newspaper made me realise how lucky I'd been. When I left, a fight had broken out between the Romanian guy and Jimmy. The huge Romanian ended up in hospital with serious head wounds. My new Scottish friend had battered him with an iron bar. He was charged with GBH. He was probably looking at another three-year stretch or more. Oh well, as daft as it sounds, I was glad for him. He was better off in there, off the booze and safe. That could have been me lying in that hospital bed or sitting in a police cell. There are no laws to protect you when you're homeless after dark. You're alone, exposed and vulnerable. That night, feeling defeated, I'd had to settle for a stinking urine-drenched doorway again. "Welcome to the Mad House!"

A few more days had passed, ground hog day again. It was just the weather that changed. It was starting to get dark. I'd decided to sit and wait for the supermarket to reduce the prices on their almost out of date stock, so I could spend the few pence I'd got from begging earlier. I sat on a bench nearby and waited, along with a few others who had the same idea. I think they were always there about this time every night. I needed to get in there in front of them. It was sort of like Black Friday for the homeless. The only difference being, this was nearly every day and you weren't fighting over a forty-two inch TV, it was more like a ten inch, out of date pizza. While I was waiting I must have drifted off to sleep and when I woke up the supermarket was closed. To make matters worse, my Bergen had been stolen. I now had no sleeping bag or tent and no ten-inch pizza, the fucking scumbags! All I had left was what I stood up in. There was no one around; who ever it was that took my gear had long gone. I bet it was those fucking wankers who had been sitting nearby. I put my head in my hands. I thought I'd hit rock bottom before; I certainly had now. It was going to be a cold one tonight.

'Are you looking for this?' came a voice from behind me.

I recognised that voice. I looked around, it was Tom, he'd sneaked up behind me, and he was holding my Bergen.

'Tom, where the hell did you come from?'

'I was walking past and I saw this guy asleep, so I thought I'd take his stuff, to teach him a lesson,' said Tom.

He sat down next to me. I could tell by the look on his face that I was about to get either a lecture or a telling off.

'The first lesson in tramp-ism' began Tom, 'is never fall asleep on a bench outside a supermarket where everyone can see you, especially around here. Next time, if you want to kip on a bench, sit up and look like you're reading a book or waiting for the bus or something and make sure you've got a firm grip on your gear.'

I was glad to see him and get my stuff back. I didn't need the fucking lecture though. But he carried on regardless. It was great to see him and have someone to talk to.

'It's a cold one, where are you sleeping tonight?' I asked.

'How long have you been out here now, three or four weeks? You youngsters don't know what it means to be cold. To wake up on a park bench at two in the morning, knowing you won't be able to get warm until the sun comes up, that's cold.' replied Tom.

'You're wrong Tom, I was in the army remember. A few nights piss wet through, standing in a waterlogged trench on Salisbury Plains or freezing my bollocks off in the Brecon Beacons, was much worse.'

'Fair play, you got me there. Salisbury Plains, that brings back memories,' he said.

'Oh, you know Salisbury plains then.'

'Been there a few times, yes.'

Even though it was a bitterly cold night, it didn't put Tom off his drink. He took a swig from his can of lager and then offered me some.

'No thanks,' I said, 'how can you drink that stuff on a night like this?'

'Easy,' said Tom, 'it warms you up. It puts fire in your belly.'

'How have you been Tom, what have you been up to?'

'It's a long story,' said Tom, 'come on grab your gear, let's get out of here.'

'Where to?'

'I know a nice warm and dry place we can go,' he replied.

Tom's drink of choice was lager, one of the most popular drinks for homeless people and tramps, mainly because it's cheap and gets the job done. That night was one of the coldest nights of the year. Tom suggested we head for a nearby church hall, which opened as an emergency shelter on nights when the temperature dropped below freezing. Being friends with Tom was already starting to pay dividends. Ten minutes later we arrived at the church. I was glad we'd finally arrived; my feet had gone numb with the cold.

'Do you think we'll get in Tom?' I asked, worried we may be turned away.

'We'll be ok, even though we're not wearing ties. I'll have a word with the doorman, plus I know the DJ. Act sober and let me do the talking.'

'What?' Tom was sometimes miles ahead of me with his sense of humour.

We were in luck. The staff greeted us inside with a smile. There were several camp beds made up on the floor and we managed to get the last two. Looking around the church there were people sleeping everywhere. We gladly helped ourselves to the donated food of soup and bread and returned to our camp beds. Relieved to get out the cold, we both lay on our beds and started to chat.

'We're in luck tonight Andy, it's hard to get in here. There's usually someone from Alcoholics Anonymous and Drug rehab here, giving you the waffle, advice and stuff. It must be too cold for them tonight.'

'So how did you get on in court Tom?'

'Hundred and twenty quid fine, plus a eighty quid victim surcharge, I didn't bloody touch him. If anyone was a victim it was me, that kebab made me ill. I don't know when they expect me to pay that fine, I wish them luck on that one.'

'Oh, by the way Tom, thanks for that twenty quid, you didn't have to do that.'

Tom looked at me as though I'd lost the plot and said 'what twenty quid? I don't know what you're talking about'.

'I'll pay you back when I can' I said.

'Listen,' said Tom, 'it was a reward for giving me my wallet back, intact, you deserved it ok.'

'And your dog, you didn't get it back then, I take it.'

'He's still on death row. They said they'd look after him for me, until I got out.'

'Out of where?' I asked, wondering if he'd been arrested again.

'Hospital, I went to get that cough sorted out, like you told me to, and they admitted me for a few days. It must have been bad because they put me through all sorts of stupid tests. I'll tell you what though, after they'd hosed me down and disinfected my bollocks, I had a great time. I loved being waited on and pampered by all the nurses it was great. They spoke all sorts of languages, some even spoke English.'

'So, you're ok now then?'

'I think so. I didn't hang around to find out, no news is good news, as they say. I feel better though.'

'Good. But I've noticed you still have the cough, you should have stayed there to find out what was up with you.'

'Lesson number two,' said Tom 'never out stay your welcome as far as hospitals are concerned, it can be a downward cycle, a revolving door between the streets and the hospital, until you never come out.'

'What do you mean?' I asked, confused by his statement.

Tom went on to explain 'I remember a few years back, I fell over one morning and cut my head open on a bottle, while I was searching a bin outside the bus station, looking for a free breakfast and newspaper. The next thing I knew, I was in the back of a meat wagon on my way to Accident and Emergency. I lay there for ages before I was seen to. After stitching me up, they couldn't wait to get rid of me. They had enough on their hands with geriatrics and the pissed up Saturday night undesirables. The last thing they wanted was me stinking the place out and nicking their alcohol hand gel, to have later with my favourite tipple. So, I was unceremoniously discharged back out onto the streets. Drugged up with medication and hand wash gel cocktails, it wasn't long before I was back lying on the pavement again. This time my stitches had burst open; there was claret and vomit everywhere. But no one gives a shit if you're a tramp, they just said "Look, someone's collapsed, oh, it's ok everyone, he's just a tramp". Sooner or later, after I'd lost several pints of blood, a concerned member of the public who happened to be passing by noticed me. "Someone's collapsed, quick, call an ambulance!" So, I'm off to hospital again and this time it's even worse. I'm now infected, malnourished, exhausted and made to stay in for a few days. The cycle is repeated again and again until I end up nearly dead in intensive care. All that, just for a fucking pizza breakfast and a soggy three-day old copy of a newspaper. No, hospitals are not for me, I hate the places. I've lived most of my life on the streets so I'll die on the streets.'

I lay there pissing myself with laughter, listening to his exaggerated stories. He could certainly spin a good yarn.

'What about you, I thought you were giving up the streets and sorting yourself out?' he said.
'I was, but I found out it's not as easy as I thought. I don't know why I'm still here but I just am. I feel free but I'm finding it really hard to survive out here. I don't know how you do it year after year.'
'It's easy. You just need educating, that's all,' replied Tom.
'Will you teach me Tom?' I asked.

He lay looking at me for a while. I began to wonder if he would answer my question. He took a sighing breath before he spoke.

'I met someone just like you a few years ago and he asked me the same thing. People hit the streets for all sorts of reasons. I said to him are you sure this is what you want? He said yes. I taught him everything I knew. But I found out he shouldn't have been on the streets, so I'd completely wasted my time.'

'What happened to him?' I asked.

'He threw himself in front of a train. They had a job on trying to collect all the pieces I tell you. The selfish fucker never gave a thought for the unfortunate train driver. So, what I'm going to ask you now, is this, you won't go off and do something like that will you? I've got no time for time wasters.'

'You've got no worries there' I said, if I was going to do something like that, I'd have done it ages ago with what I've seen and been through.'

'It sounds like you're stuck in a rut son, don't worry, you won't be on the streets for long. As soon as someone points you in the right direction for help, you'll be off the streets in no time and a stronger person for it. Trust me, I know. Take this place, it's full of the same old faces.'

This guy, must be a veteran, only vets talk like that. What's the betting something happened to him out there, wherever out there was. That's why he walks the streets. I decided to take a chance and ask him again about his background.

'So, you did Salisbury Plains then Tom, stationed around there was you?'

'Sort of, that was a long time ago. I only look forward, I try not to look back,' he replied.

That was about as much as I got. He went quiet after that. Tom was hiding something and whatever it was must have affected him badly.

'If you really don't want me to ask you about it, I won't.'

He didn't say anything, so I thought I'd take a more humorous approach. Maybe if I got him laughing he'd be more willing to talk.

'Do you want to know what I reckon? I reckon you're Special Forces. I read in the paper, that the government has deployed so many ex SF guys undercover on the streets, to sniff out returning ISIS fighters. Apparently, they are arriving back from their crumbling caliphate in Syria and Iraq and are now trying to hide within the great unwashed. I'm right aren't I?'

'Are you on fucking crack? Replied Tom. 'Yes, you're right. We all meet up at the food banks every Saturday for our weekly Intel Brief. Don't go pissing on Tom when you stagger out of your night club on a Saturday night as you may get a big surprise and it won't be a bottle of cider bearing down on your bonce, it'll be a lethal punch to the throat, Endex.'

'You're ok Tom, your secret's safe with me.'

Tom started to laugh. At least we ended the evening laughing.

'Goodnight Andy.'
'Goodnight Tom.'

CHAPTER 7

The next morning, we were back on the streets and heading for the RSPCA, or death row as Tom likes to call it, to rescue the dog with no name. On the way, Tom didn't waste any time and started to teach me more about the art of tramp-ism, I think he was enjoying it.

'Part of the requirements for the 1st Volunteer Beggar's Battalion, is to be in possession of a sad looking dog. It's your alarm clock, your early warning system, friend and begging aid. He's your Swiss army knife for street life.'

On arrival at the RSPCA, his far from sad dog was waiting for him. I must admit his dog looked a lot better than it did a few weeks ago. They must have spoilt it like hell in there. It was an emotional re-union; the dog's reaction on seeing his owner was a beautiful moment. He could barely contain his excitement as he ran up to Tom and then started rushing around him, then sinking to the floor overwhelmed with joy at seeing his owner again. The dog then jumped up into Tom's arms and started to lick his face. He was either excited to see Tom again or he wanted to give his tramp owner a good wash.

We were soon out on the street. Tom tied his dog to a piece of string and off we went.

'Are you going to tell me the name of your dog Tom?'

'Wolfgang.'

'Wolfgang, why Wolfgang?'

'Because he's a sausage dog.'

'Hold on, I get it. Wolfgang. You were in, Germany, weren't you?' My uncle used to tell me stories about him, when he served as part of the British Army of the Rhine. He said Wolfgang was a legend. When the army was on exercise, he'd just appear out of nowhere, driving his little blue snack wagon, selling his bratwurst sausages, chips and lager to the troops around the training area.'

'Don't forget the yellow handbags... yellow boxes of Herforder lager,' Tom added.

'Yes, he mentioned them too,' I said.

'So how long were you posted out there, Tom?'

'Five years, anyway I thought you wanted to learn about tramp-ism?'

'I do.'

Again, he declined to talk about his service, why? Most squaddies would always pull up a sandbag about their army career. It was starting to do my head in. I knew next to nothing about him, apart from his name and service number, and I only knew that from finding the ID card in his wallet. The few short conversations we'd had also told me of two places he had been stationed.

'So, what else are you going to teach me today Tom?'

Tom replied 'This morning, we're going to wander around the shopping centre, grovelling for pennies with Wolfgang.'

'I tried that there yesterday with no luck, they just took the piss out of me. All I got was sixty-five pence for my troubles, and that was after four hours. I said to one guy 'Can you spare twenty pence please? I'm homeless.' He said, "You won't find a house for twenty pence around here mate," and walked away.

'I've heard them all over the years,' Tom said. The best one I can remember is when I was sitting outside the tube station in London. This guy came walking up to me holding a Big Mac and a cup of coffee. At first, I thought it was my birthday, thinking he was going to give them to me. "Are you, hungry mate?" he said, smiling. 'Yes, I'm starving,' I replied with a smile.' "Well, I don't usually help your kind out, but it's your lucky day." He got down on one knee and pointed down the road. "About a hundred yards down there you'll probably find the gherkin that I chucked from this burger a few seconds ago."

'The wanker, what did you do? I would have knocked him out,' I said.

'I decided I'd just laugh at him, he didn't expect that. I think he thought that because I was a tramp my brain would be too fucked up to have a sense of humour. It's best not to bite in those situations. It will just get you down and you'll start losing the will to live. In that incident, he gave me a two quid and said, "Here, go and get yourself a Happy Meal." 'Begging is a fine art. Most people don't give a shit about a smelly tramp and take a wide berth, but, if you have a cute little dog, some people will just melt on the spot. And having a dog that limps is even better.'

'But Wolfgang hasn't got a limp,' I said 'what're you talking about?'

'He will have, when I kick the hell out of him.'

'What! No you fucking don't,' I said, feeling protective of the little dog.

Tom got down on one knee to stroke his dog. 'Relax, I wouldn't do that to you, would I Wolfgang, no. Wolfgang, vet,' Tom said. 'Good boy.'

And would you believe it, Wolfgang started to limp. He'd taught his bloody dog to limp on the command 'vet.' I'd never seen anything like it. Minutes later, there we were in the shopping centre.

'Excuse me madam; you couldn't spare a few pence, could you? I'm trying to raise money, so I can take my poor dog to the vet,' Tom said, to a young woman pushing a pram.

Hearing the command 'vet', Wolfgang jumped up and started to limp. His performance was even more convincing when he looked up at the woman with sad eyes and gave a little whimper. I just cracked up laughing in the background; the dog deserved an Oscar.

'Oh, the poor thing, look at him, that's so sad. What happened?' the woman asked, bending forward to stroke him.

'He got hit by a bus, it was the driver's fault, but he's a dog, no one cares do they Wolfgang. There are some cruel people out there.' Tom was really laying it on. His performance was every bit as good as Wolfgang's.

Within twenty minutes, Tom had made over a tenner in change and we were on the move.

'Why didn't you keep going?' I asked.

'You can have too much of a good thing, better to quit while you're ahead. Look at that security guard, over there on your right, he's on his radio, we've been rumbled, let's go.'

We left the shopping centre and headed for the chip shop. At least we'd all have something warm to eat today.

'Wow, that was great, why don't you do that more often.' I still couldn't believe how much money we'd made in such a short period of time.

'If I did that everyday don't you think eventually people would catch on? Before you know it, Wolfgang and me would be a YouTube sensation. And then everyone would know our scam.'

'Eh, if you train him to do other things, then you could enter Britain's Got Talent. Err Tom, your dog's still limping.'

'Yes, everything has its flaws. I haven't got a command for that yet, give him a few days and he'll be back to normal.'

I couldn't shut him up all day. It was like I was his pupil. I never knew there was so much to learn about living on the streets. It was getting late. We headed for one of Tom's usual stops, in one of the many hospital bus shelters. We sat down, happy with our day's work, chatting and drinking lager while watching the world go by.

The last bus came and went. As the bus shelter was on the hospital grounds, Tom told me that it was usually about now we'd end up getting moved on by one of the hospital security guards.

'But you never know, we might get lucky. They might feel sorry for us and bring us out a hot drink. It all depends who is on shift tonight.' he said.

'Check out Wolfgang, it looks like he's found his spot for the night,' I said, watching him take a piss up the side of the shelter. 'He's marking his territory.'

'Dogs are clever. They mark their territory to tell everyone it's theirs. Imagine, if people did that the homeless would own everything. Do you reckon if we piss all over this bus shelter, no one would come near us?' Tom joked.

'No one is going to come near it anyway Tom, we stink.'

'So, have you decided to take up tramping as a career yet?' he asked.

'I'm considering it,' I replied, laughing.

'Everyone knows there's a downside of becoming a member of the great unwashed, but just think about the benefits,' Tom said.

'Like what?'

'For a starter, free food and accommodation. You don't have to change your socks as much as you used to. No worries about the price of petrol, because that burnt out Fiesta you slept in last night to keep you dry, isn't going anywhere. No rent to pay, no fucker to buy Christmas presents for, and a free slap up Christmas dinner, turkey, Christmas pudding, the works, laid on by the local Sally Army or RBL. No shaving.'

I was expecting him to stop, but he just kept on reeling them out.

'And you are more or less permanently pissed, rendering hangovers a thing of the past. You don't have to pick a fight with anyone. You can shadow box with your reflection in shop doorways and nobody gets hurt. Unlimited travel all around the country. We are virtually fucking invisible, hidden away. We don't vote; don't pay taxes, own homes or credit cards. The truth is we've been swept under the carpet, we don't exist.'

'You can shut up now Tom, you've sold it to me.'

That night the security left us alone and we even got woken up around five in the morning with a nice cuppa. I think it was their way of saying drink up; it's time to leave. There was no lay in. They told us to move on before the bus service started. We gathered our few bits together and headed back to the town centre.

That afternoon the weather was acting strange, it started to get unusually warm. We'd heard that there was a bit of a storm coming our way so I was starting to worry about where we were going to stay that evening. We needed somewhere better than a flimsy bus shelter or doorway. I suggested to Tom that we head out of town and tent up somewhere, but Tom wasn't even fazed by it. It was as though he already had something sorted.

'So, how many tramp miles have you done Tom, how many places have you stayed?'

'Dozens of places,' said Tom. 'I started off in London but it got too dangerous. I've heard it's even worse now with the invasion of Eastern Europeans. Some of them lot that sleep rough actually work in bars, hotels and restaurants, but they still muscle in on the homeless centres for cheap food and showers, instead of paying rent. So, I moved on. It didn't matter where I ended up; I wasn't bothered. I just saved up enough money for a bus ticket and got the fuck out of there. If you want to travel, just jump on a random out of town bus, buy a ticket and fall asleep. You're homeless anyway, so you might as well get some shelter, at least until the driver kicks you off at the last stop. Wherever you end up, that's your new home, until you've outstayed your welcome.'

'What do you mean outstayed your welcome? I asked.

'Everyone gets to know you so you start getting popular and ending up with a tramp name and then the kids go hunting for you. People get sick of the same face outside their shops. They get used to all your scams. On the other hand, when you're new in town, nobody will know you. You have that element of surprise in pastures new. You can hang around the pub, pinching half pints. The rougher the pub the better, where most of the punters are too bladdered to even realise. You might get lucky, there might be a party in the function room, with a buffet. After the partygoers have staggered off into the night, you can mine sweep all the leftovers and all those half-glasses of Christ-knows what. Before anybody realises what you're up to, you'll be long gone, half pissed, with a plate full of prawn sandwiches, sausage rolls and cheese on sticks. Plus, you're able to find all sorts of new places to sleep.'

'What about tonight, Tom, where are we sleeping? We can't stay here, you can share my tent if you want?'

'No, you're ok, me and Wolfgang are already fixed up for tonight, aren't we boy, fingers crossed. I don't want to be sleeping out here in some tent, with what's on its way. No thanks,' Tom replied.

'So, now you're a weatherman as well Tom. What is on its way?'

'No, I'm not, but it comes with living out on the streets all these years, knowing when bad weather is coming.'

It started to get windy, you could tell there was something brewing. A storm was coming alright. If I was going to pitch my tent, it would need to be somewhere sheltered. I tried to recall the places I'd previously visited.

'You're quite welcome to join us if you want,' Tom said, bringing me back to the present.

'Thanks, that's kind of you Tom. Where do you have in mind? The Holiday Inn or the Ritz, maybe,' I answered sarcastically.

'Not quite. You'll see, come on, let's go.'

Where to now I thought. This guy had so many tricks up his sleeve. I followed Tom to the local corner shop. With what was left of the tenner that we'd got from Wolfgang's Oscar winning performance the day before in the shopping centre, plus my measly sixty-five pence, we managed to buy six cans of cheap lager, a small bag of dog food and a large bag of chips, from the chip shop next door. Off we trundled to Tom's secret location, eating our chips on the way.

CHAPTER 8

It was Friday night. There weren't many people around. It must have been due to the approaching storm and it was starting to get really windy. We arrived at an old cricket pavilion just outside town, near the church we had stayed in a few days ago. I was amazed when Tom promptly took out a key to let himself in a side door. We entered the building, it was cold inside but it was out of the elements. We couldn't really explore the place as it was too dark and putting the light on would give us away. There was a row of houses not too far away so all it needed was some neighbourhood watch do-gooder to alert the local plod. After locking the door behind us, we found a clear spot on the floor and made ourselves comfortable. We could just about see each other, thanks to the distant street lights shining through a small window.

'You kept this quiet Tom, how long have you been coming here, it's not bad is it?'

'This is the first night,' he replied. 'When we stayed at the church the other night I went for a wander round while you were sleeping and saw this key hanging on the notice board, in the vicar's office. I thought that wasn't a very secure place for a key, so I put it in my pocket for safe keeping. It had cricket pavilion written on the tag. Seeing as this is the only pavilion for miles around I guessed this would be it. I can't see many sporting activities happening around here this weekend, with the weather being shit. So, I reckon we're ok till at least Monday. I nearly forgot I had it. My memory is getting worse you know.'

'That's theft. You'll go to hell Tom, especially nicking a key from a church.'

'As long as there's an off licence down there, I'll be happy thanks.'

I was soon inside my sleeping bag. Tom had Wolfgang to keep him warm and his layers of clothing of course. Tom didn't need a sleeping bag; with that many layers of clothing on he was like an onion. The problem was, he also smelt like an onion. Unbuttoning his coat, he revealed a collection of cardigans, jumpers, shirts and vests, all in various colours. He must have had about twelve layers of clothes on. He looked like a cricket umpire on a very cold day.

'So how did you end up with Wolfgang, Tom?'

'I found him on the street, abused and abandoned. I was homeless, he was homeless, and now we have each other. He's everything to me.' Tom started to scratch Wolfgang's ears and gave him a kiss on the nose. 'Aren't you, you daft dog.'

'This place needs a name. I know, how about Uncle Tom's cabin,' I suggested.

We began to laugh, then Tom's laugh turned into a coughing fit. He doubled over, coughing away and his face turned almost purple. I began to get worried.

'Are you, ok mate?' I asked, concerned about him.

He cleared his throat and started to laugh, 'I'm fine.' he said in a gravelly voice.

I passed him one of his lagers. 'Here get that down your neck. So, you don't bother with a sleeping bag then?'

'Proper tramps don't use sleeping bags' replied Tom. 'Only the homeless use sleeping bags. To tell you the truth, some years ago, I did use a sleeping bag for a few weeks. Until one night, around bonfire night, some of the local kids set fire to my bag while I was trying to sleep in a doorway. I just managed to get out of it in time. I had that much alcohol in me that night that I would have lit up like a roman candle! So, ever since then I haven't bothered.'

'Thanks Tom, that's really filled me with confidence, now you've got me worried.'

'I'm just telling you, that's all. You'll have to get yourself a big coat like me. **There's no respect for proper tramps anymore, they're a dying breed. Your traditional tramps of the seventies and eighties would sit at the side of the road, knocking back cheap cider, meths or white spirits.** You don't see that anymore. The ones that danced for you, shouting at you in a drunken slur, they've nearly all gone now.'

'So, you like to think you're one of a dying breed then Tom?'

'Yes, why not. All you've got now is smack-heads and the drunken antics of young kids out of their faces on a Friday and Saturday night. You try getting a free room in the cells on those nights, you've got no chance; it's all changed now sadly. Then you've got the poor sods with mental health problems and people like us who chose to be on the streets. You don't really want this life do you Andy? **A young man like you wanting to live like this, stepping over** disgusting bodies, the lowest of humanity slumped in the doorways, smelling of booze, piss and vomit. And when you try to help them, they just want to fight you, I bet you didn't think it could ever be that bad?'

'I don't know, living in the barracks wasn't all bad Tom,' I said.

We both laughed. Wolfgang managed to squeeze in between us, wagging his tail as he glanced from Tom to me.

'You were going to tell me how you ended up on the streets,' Tom said, as he absent-mindedly stroked Wolfgang.

'Do you really want to know Tom?'

We cracked open another lager and I decided to let it all out and tell him. I'd never really told anyone the full story; maybe it would help me.

'Ok, you win but it's not much of a story really and you've probably heard it all before anyway. Time to start the violins...I loved my time in the army and I wish I was back in. I did two tours of Afghanistan. I saw some shit, like most of us who went out there, but it didn't bother me like it did some of them. PTSD isn't the reason I'm out here on the streets, at least I don't think it is, but that might come later. It was just a bad set of circumstances. I got married while I was in the army, but she wouldn't move into married quarters so she stayed in Derby. We were very happy at first, until we tried for kids, without any luck. She blamed it on the army. How could we try for a baby, with me being away all the time? So, I gave in and got out. I had to if I wanted to save my marriage. After I left, things started to go south rapidly. Everything began to change, she started to get all bitter and nasty as the months went by with no sign of pregnancy. Then she started to see someone else behind my back, while I was at work. I tried to pretend it wasn't happening and that I didn't care, but it hit me hard. Then one day she just came out with it. "I'm leaving you Andy," there was no emotion in her voice; she'd made her mind up. She moved in with her mum at first. I thought I'd give her a few days and she'll be back. But I was wrong; it was just a stepping-stone. She moved in with him within a week. I found out later why she moved in with him so quickly. She was having his baby. I had a lot of time off work with stress and started gambling on gaming machines just to escape from it all. Eventually I lost my job and was on that slippery slope downwards. My gambling habit got worse and my money ran out. I couldn't find another job, not even a shite job just to pay the bills. She walked away with nearly everything and I was left with virtually jack shit, apart from the debts. The bills stopped being paid, electricity, gas, water, the council tax, everything. Creditors started banging on the door and bailiffs came around, taking away what was left of my possessions. The landlord was giving me grief about the unpaid rent. I managed to borrow some money from friends. I put the money in the bank to pay the arrears, but because I was overdrawn, it was swallowed up; I complained to the bank but they didn't listen. Eventually, the landlord wanted me out.'

'You could have claimed benefits surely,' said Tom.

'I tried. What a fucking minefield that was, filling in form after form. To get any money out of them, they want you to jump through hoops and that's only if you've filled the forms in correctly. If you're lucky you might get a few quid in six weeks. By then, the system has changed yet again. So you have to go through the whole process again and again. I started to look around for a cheap bedsit, but with a credit history worth shit and not a chance of finding a deposit, I knew my days were numbered. I didn't hang around when they came to evict me that morning. I grabbed my Bergen, doss bag and tent and hit the streets. I was gone. Walking down the road that morning, for the first time in ages, the pressure had lifted, it felt like I was back in the army for a moment and I was off on exercise, this was going to be easy, I thought.'

'Why didn't you go to the council and tell them you were homeless, they would have given you a room at a hostel or something, that's how it works isn't it?' said Tom.

'I didn't want a home. I just wanted to hide away. I didn't want to be helped.'

After a pause, Tom gave me his response. I was hoping for a little bit of sympathy perhaps. I should have known better.

'Well, that was fucking boring,' he said.

That's military for you. I didn't know how to react to that, it was something between laughing my head off or knocking his head off. I just laughed it off and then I just lay there for a moment. Even though it was a while back, it was all still very fresh in my mind and the reason I was lying on this wooden floor. One minute I had everything, looking forward to a great future, then the next minute bang, it was all gone. It's funny what life throws at you.

'Eh, chin up soldier boy,' said Tom 'I was joking, I feel for you. You'll be over it soon. Then you'll look back and say what the fuck was that all about.'

'What time are we getting up Tom, we don't want to overlay do we?'

I was worried that someone may come in to clean the building. At least if we were awake early, we could make a quick exit.

'There's no chance of that happening with Wolfgang around, is there boy,' said Tom, as he cuddled his dog.

Wolfgang had a sort of wake-up dance he did in the mornings, where he'd lick the hell out of your face. It was his way of telling you he needed a dump and some food and water. The next morning, when Wolfgang did his dance, we just ignored him because we weren't going anywhere. It was still lashing down with rain outside and very windy. I doubted anyone would bother coming to clean this place while the weather was bad. Spring was on the way. The shit weather made the decision for us and we had a lay in.

At half past ten Tom was still asleep. I climbed out of my sleeping bag, trying my best not to disturb him. I should have realised I was wasting my time; Tom had an inbuilt radar for any movement.

'Where are you going?' Tom asked, sitting up. Wolfgang jumped up, started to pant and lick Tom's face, wagging his tail. He was ready for his breakfast.

'That's it Wolfgang, get stuck in, he needs a good wash anyway,' I said, laughing.

'Wolfgang no, do you have to?' Tom said, trying to bury his head in his coat.

'I'm off on a quick recce to see what's around, and we need a piss don't we Wolfgang. Go back to sleep Tom. I'll see if I can find him some water to have with his dog biscuits.'

'You won't find anything in here, apart from a load of jock straps,' Tom replied, as he drifted back off to sleep.

It wasn't long before I was back with two piping hot

cups of tea, some out of date custard cream biscuits and Wolfgang's water.

'Wakey wakey, there you go Tom,' I said, offering him a cup of tea and biscuits.

Tom sat up with a look of surprise on his face.

'Am I dreaming? Is that a cup of tea and how did you know they were my favourite biscuits?'

'There's a kitchen next door. Why wouldn't there be? It's a cricket pavilion, cucumber sandwiches and all that. Sorry, no milk though.'

'That's ok, I'm not complaining.'

'And another thing, this place gets better. I've just felt the radiators and they're on, they must have known we were coming.'

'I thought it was getting warmer. Fucking hell, breakfast in bed, central heating, what next,' Tom laughed.

'I've found something else as well.'

Tom looked on with anticipated excitement on his face. 'Go on,' he said.

'I've found the changing rooms, and you know what comes with changing rooms… Showers! We can have a shower Tom, how good is that.'

His facial expression changed to a look of horror. Anyone seeing him would think I'd just offered him a poisoned chalice.

'Err, now that's going too far. Granted, a little bit of luxury, once in a while, is ok, but we're tramps, we don't take showers. 'The Book of Tramp-ism,' Chapter four, section three. Not at any time will a tramp take a shower or bath to cleanse their body. And what's the point anyway, afterwards we'd only have to put all these dirty clothes back on again.'

'That's where you're wrong Tom. We don't have to, I found some other things as well'

I left the room and returned with two full sets of cricket whites. 'Take your pick, there's loads hung up in there, all shapes and sizes.'

'We can't walk round town wearing them,' said Tom. 'People will think we're advertising a new wash powder.'

'Why not, we just need something to wear until our clothes get dry on the radiators. Come on Tom, get them off.'

'Oh, for fuck's sake,' Tom replied.

It took me a while to persuade him, but in the end, he gave in. It wasn't long before we were sitting on the floor of the shower room, stark bollock naked, scrubbing ourselves, and washing our stinking clothes with a large brush and washing up liquid, whilst being blasted by twelve power showers, aimed straight at us. It felt like we were sitting inside a submarine that had just been hit and was sinking, even Wolfgang joined in. He began chasing around after random bubbles.

'You know what, this is fucking crazy. I haven't had this much fun for years,' Tom said smiling.

After we'd showered, we dried ourselves on some old tablecloths, put on our cricket whites and placed all our tramp clothes on the radiators in the function room. Then we spent the rest of the day waiting for them to dry. The weather now was at its peak, but we didn't care, we were as warm as toast. Before we knew it, it was getting dark again. We helped ourselves to another cup of tea, finished off the custard creams and retired to our sleeping area; it had been a great day. We were really starting to bond. It was the same sort of bond you get in the military. A second night of banter began.

'All good things come to an end Andy, we need to be out of here by tomorrow.'

'I know mate, but at least we'll be nice and clean for a while, after that shower.'

'As I said' proceeded Tom 'this goes against all the rules of being a tramp you know. It's important that extra layer of dirt, it's like having an extra layer of skin protecting you from the elements. It's like tramp varnish. I'm missing it already.'

'Don't worry, I won't mention it to your trampy mates, I wouldn't want to ruin your reputation. Look on the bright side. You've just killed off all those little friends who were hitching a free ride on that coat of yours and there's nothing wrong with having a little time out. We can go back to being tramps tomorrow.'

Suddenly, lightening lit up the room, and then a loud rumble of thunder reverberated through the building. Wolfgang started to shake, and pressed himself close to Tom, who talked to him, rubbing his back to calm him down.

'Wolfgang sometimes has panic attacks at night, especially when it thunders, don't you boy. I think it's a result of all that abuse he suffered as a pup. I found him wandering the streets you know.'

It was obvious that Wolfgang brought joy to Tom's heart. But it was more than that, Wolfgang brought purpose, he gave Tom a reason to get up every day.

'Do you like dogs, Andy?'

'I didn't like dogs until I bumped into Wolfgang,' I answered, truthfully.

Tom went on to tell me about his first meeting with

Wolfgang and how it didn't go too well. As he spoke, he continued to stroke Wolfgang, who shook and whimpered with each peal of thunder.

'He was standoffish at first; a bit unsure whether he could trust me. But all that changed when I pulled some broken biscuits out of my pocket. He started to nibble them out of my hand, then let his tail do the talking. He's my companion; we're together twenty-four seven, apart from when I have to go to the hospital. it was my final visit last week.'

'You're ok now then?' I asked.

'Of course, I'm ok. I was given the all clear. I told you, this cough is just the street cough, and everyone gets it. You'll get it eventually, that's why you have to get yourself sorted young man.'

I didn't believe Tom. He wasn't all right. He was losing weight and sleeping more and more. You couldn't tell him though because he'd just shut up shop like he does when I quiz him on his military service. We chatted for a while about the different people he'd met on his travels.

'Have you ever met anyone else like Yogi?' I asked, remembering the man mountain I'd fought with.

'Plenty, you get them in every town you go to. I met this homeless guy in Nottingham, he seemed normal at first, until he told me that there were pterodactyls everywhere, he was convinced they were going to take over the world.'

'Maybe he knew something you didn't,' I joked.

'And there was another guy in Chesterfield, he was totally not right in the head. He called himself 'The Chicken King.' He used to pace up and down the road making clucking noises, clapping loudly while doing a chicken walk, with the same head movements as a chicken, and then he'd start asking passers-by to pay his chicken tax. When he wasn't collecting taxes, he had another side. He'd get aggressive and shout at cars in the street. I heard he got run over dozens of times. Oh, and you'll like this one. There was one old guy when I was in London, he must have been in his sixties, an ex RSM or something. He would regularly be seen walking up the high street complete with beret, blazer, swagger stick and highly polished ammo boots. Most days he'd be shitfaced, standing in the street, telling every fucker to keep off the grass and stop sitting on the walls. And if he caught you with your hands in your pockets, he'd have a fit. His favourite hangout was the local pub. He always asked for a glass of coke, because he said he was on duty. But everyone knew he'd been in the bog topping up his glass of coke with brandy from his hip flask, and if he got caught he'd say, 'don't tell the Colonel will you. Another one of his pastimes was he'd always salute the girls walking by and be willing to pull up his shirt to show them his machine gun bullet hole scars. He'd tell the girls he got them from the Argies in the Falkland's, but the truth is they were the result of a motorbike accident. His downfall came one day when he showed one of the girls a little bit more than his so-called battle wounds. It turned out she was only fifteen and her six foot five dad was walking behind her. God knows where he is now.'

'Don't you think we should be a little bit more sympathetic towards these characters, who nobody seems to care for?' I hope I never end up like the people Tom spoke about.

'Nah, don't you mean someone should be going around with a nine millimetre putting the poor fuckers out of their misery.'

'You don't mean that, do you?' I asked, shocked.

'No, of course I don't... just the odd few, like the guy they used to call The Devil. He used to walk up to you and make the sign of the cross on your forehead and say shit like, 'you are going to die in seven days.' He did it to me once, he scared the shit out of me.'

'And did you die?'

'Obviously not, but it did freak me out for the next seven days. I kept well away from buses. I know we aren't supposed to mock the afflicted, and they have genuine problems, but fucking hell, they sometimes get up to some funny shit!'

Tom started to cough. He reached over and took a long swig from a hip flask he'd been hiding under his hat. His hat was the only thing he had refused to wash earlier.

'That's better, I needed that.'

'You kept that quiet Tom.'

'It's my emergency brandy supply, do you want a swig.'

'Nah, you're ok.'

I was going to quiz him on how he became a tramp, like he had quizzed me the previous night but I'd already been bawled at twice. The last thing I wanted to do was lose the bond we were building. I needed him and I think he needed me. I could tell he was struggling.

I woke up the next morning, Sunday, around nine. I hadn't slept so well in weeks, but something had disturbed me. I thought it must have been Tom snoring, or maybe Wolfgang whimpering in his sleep?

'Tom, wake up mate, we need to move on. And by the way, your alarm clock dog didn't go off again, you need to fix it.'

'Didn't I tell you, he doesn't do Sundays, I taught him Sunday is lie in day.'

'Shut up you daft old bugger.'

Hearing us talking, Wolfgang woke up and decided to start licking Tom's face off again.

'Give over dog,' Tom said, pushing him away.

It had been so hot in the night that we'd both peeled off our whites leaving ourselves stark bollock naked. I headed for the main function room to collect our nice clean clothes from the radiators. Opening the double doors, I suddenly froze. I got the shock of my life. There I stood, naked, with my early morning wood sticking out like the Blackpool Tower, flashing myself to around thirty middle aged women.

'SHIT!!! Sorry ladies...' I stuttered, trying to cover myself with my hands.

Then Tom arrived behind me, tripping over while trying to get his pants on. The women all just sat there in silence. I think they were in shock. Some covered their eyes, others looked like they were about to scream, but most of them couldn't get enough of us. There were also some big ladies amongst them who looked like they were about to rip us apart.

'What now Andy?' Tom asked. He had managed to get one leg in his pants, before noticing the women.

'I think we're in deep shit Tom.'

Before I could say a word, one of them stood up and spoke to the other women.

'This is the ladies bowling club monthly meeting. Who booked these strippers, is this some kind of joke?'

At the same time, while unsuccessfully trying to hide

our man-hoods, we desperately gathered up all our clothes.

'Just give us a few seconds ladies and we'll be out of here.' I said, to the glowering women.

We grabbed all our clothes and headed for the toilets, we didn't hang around. The women were banging on the toilet door and they sounded really angry. We were soon dressed and gone before the police arrived or any handbag-swinging posse had formed. It was a good job the toilet had a door to the outside, as I didn't fancy trying to climb through the windows or take our chances fighting past the women. We got half a mile down the road before we rested. We were both breathing out of our arses after our sprint from the building. I think Wolfgang enjoyed the run, judging by how fast he was wagging his tail.

'Well, that was fun Tom,' I said, breathlessly.

Tom, after a short coughing fit, replied. 'For a minute there, I thought I was an ISIS terrorist and I'd just blown myself up and they were the virgin's I'd been promised.'

Humour in the midst of battle.... Brilliant I thought. I was glad Tom could see the funny side of our predicament.

'If that were the case, you'd have been well disappointed, wouldn't you? There were a few big units amongst that lot. There wasn't a virgin in sight, I can tell you that Tom.'

'Beggars can't be choosers, Andy.'

'You mean tramps.'

We both laughed as we walked down the road to anywhere. That day would stay in my memory for a long time. It had been a brilliant few days, filled with laughter and comradeship.

CHAPTER 9

A few more weeks had gone by. I was still learning new stuff every day but Tom's health seemed to be getting worse. He'd have his bad days and his good. The good weather helped him a little. I kept insisting he go to the doctors but I got the usual negative response. It was now the beginning May, still a little chilly at night, but pleasant in the day. I'd been on the streets nearly four months.

Today was Sunday, a day of rest, but not for us, we were up and about early. The clothes we had washed a few weeks ago had seen better days and had started to smell again. Heading for the River Derwent with a washboard and stone wasn't an option. My coat had had it. If it wasn't for Tom patching up the tears and holes for me, using the gaffer tape and sewing kit he carried in his Aladdin's cave of a coat, it would have fallen apart weeks ago. Tom suggested it was time we took a trip to a car boot sale, to get me fixed up with a new one.

'What about you Tom, I think you could do with a new coat too. If you took that thing off, it would walk to the skip on its own.'

Tom being Tom, he was having none of it.

'Not a chance, I've spent years sewing hidden pockets in this coat, it's part of me. I'll be buried in this coat and hat, all I need is a decent pair of trousers.'

Every Sunday morning at seven o'clock, fully laden cars would start arriving at the Derby cattle market to sell their junk at the weekly car boot sale. We arrived late to avoid paying an entrance fee. It wasn't long before we were walking up and down the rows of paste tables, occasionally stopping when something caught our eye. We decided to split up and meet up again ten minutes later.

'Did you see anything you liked Andy?' Tom asked, when we met up again.

'There is a coat I like over there, Tom. I wanted to take a closer look, but the stallholder told me to do one.'

'That's because you stink like a dead badger's arse, Andy.'

'Speak for yourself, you smelly old bastard,' I replied. 'It's taken months and months of tramping to perfect a smell like ours.' said Tom. 'Smelling like a dead animal does have its advantages sometimes. Here, look after Wolfgang and watch the master at work.'

Tom approached the stall where I had seen the coat I liked and he was soon in sniffing range...

'Not you again, if you're not going to buy anything piss off will you,' Barked the stallholder, who wasn't very happy to see Tom.

'I beg your pardon, not me again? I take it you are referring to my friend Andy. He's got scabies you know.'

'Did you hear me. You all look the bloody same anyway.'

'It's a free country,' said Tom. 'I can stand where I want.'

Tom started looking through the piles of clothes, forcing other customers to give him a wide berth, he then started coughing all over everyone so they soon began to drift away.

'Now look what you've done! All my customers are leaving!' shouted the now enraged stallholder.

'It must be your clothes mate,' Tom replied.

'You cheeky twat, if you don't piss off I'll... '

Tom called me over, beckoning me with his hand as well.

'Andy, will you come over here a minute.'

I started to walk over. The stallholder started to look agitated. He obviously didn't like the thought of two tramps sorting through his clothes.

'Look, just take whatever you want, and go will you,' he said.

Within an hour I was sorted, and Tom got some trousers. We even bought a bag of bones for Wolfgang. We walked away well pleased with our day's work, and for me, the new coat came in handy for our next scam.

I dumped my old coat and put on my new 'modified' one. For the first time in a while I looked normal. It was out with the old and in with the new. Tom had spent a couple of hours sewing hidden pockets inside the lining. He was a wizard with a needle and thread; I wondered where he'd learned to sew like that. I didn't bother asking, as I knew I was unlikely to get an answer.

In this scam he taught me, I was to be his partner in crime. We were heading for virgin territory, to a shop we'd never been in before. Tom had a great way of getting them to part with free food and booze. With it being a Sunday, there was no point trying to beg, as there weren't enough people around, but we were short on supplies, so we cut out the middle man and went straight to the source. After tying Wolfgang up outside, we entered the busy shop. Tom headed for the back of the shop, and then I came in a minute later. After picking up a pint of milk I headed straight for the counter to alert the shopkeeper.

'Watch him mate, he looks like a rough sleeper. I think he may have had a few drinks too many, or he's on something. You need to get him out mate.' I said to the shopkeeper.

Tom was now struggling to get one of the fridges open. He started to knock stuff over. Tins of beans that had been artfully stacked tumbled down and rolled across the shop floor.

'Whoops, sorry, what the fuck is up with this door? It won't open!' Tom called out at the top of his voice.

The shopkeeper was soon on his case. He hurried from behind the counter and headed towards Tom. He tried to shoo him to the front of the shop and out of the door.

'Eh, don't you shove me mate,' Tom said, digging his heels in.

'Come on you piss head druggie, out of my shop, out. **Get out of my shop! I don't want you here!'** The shopkeeper was either close to tears or ready to explode, it was hard to tell which.

While Tom was being manhandled towards the door, it was time to use his special talent. That special talent was being able to projectile vomit great distances at will. Just one more push from Mr Singh and it was game over. Tom had covered his sweet counter and most of his crisp collections with vomit. Mr Singh started to go nuts. What was once a nice clean shop, now smelt like Chernobyl on a windy day. Customers panicked trying to get out. **While all this** was going on, I was helping myself to a few bottles of drink and whatever else I could get my hands on, slipping items into one of the hidden pockets inside my rabbit warren of a coat, that Tom had transformed earlier. The shop owner was too occupied with the old tramp and his actions to notice me leaving, holding my nose, and trying my hardest not to piss myself laughing. And that's what it was like, every day a new scam. Later that afternoon we sat in the park.

'Right,' Tom said, 'let's see what we've got Andy.'

I pulled out a large packet of disposable nappies.

'What the fuck, are you serious? I'm not incontinent yet you know.'

'Sorry I thought it was a loaf of bread, I only had seconds to react, the pressure was on Tom.'

'Ok, I'll let you off with that one. More importantly, what booze did you get?'

It got worse. I then pulled out a bottle of fizzy pop.

'I'm sorry, all the spirits were behind the counter. Tom, don't look at me like that.'

Tom wasn't happy. 'You mean to say I gave up last night's pea mix for that shite? Stevie fucking Wonder could have done better than you. Ok, last chance to redeem yourself. What else have you got in there?'

Tom started to smile when I pulled out a bottle of White Lightening and a large bag of chip sticks.

'That's my boy. I'll let you off, just.'

I started to feel guilty that I'd stolen the goods. But Tom tried to reassure me, sort of!

'Stop feeling sorry for yourself Andy.'

'But I've never stolen anything in my life before this.

Sorry, that's not exactly true. I once made it out of the supermarket without paying for a carrier bag. The security guard suspected nothing.'

'I'm surprised homeless people don't steal more than they do.' Tom said.

'Because it's against the law,' I replied.

'Look at it this way, if we get away with it, great, if we don't, what's the worst that could happen? We end up in a police cell on a rubber mattress, or worse, in prison with three meals a day and perks. It's a win, win, situation. Want a chip stick?' he answered, offering me the bag.

'No thanks.'

As always, Tom had an answer for everything. Even though we needed the stuff I'd stolen, I still felt guilty about taking it.

'Why don't we just go to the food banks for food, Tom? It's a lot easier.'

'Sod that, that's for homeless people, we're tramps remember. Anyway, it takes all the fun out of it. You can't just go in there and take what you want from a food bank. You, have to get a food bank voucher. That means begging off the **advice centre** or homeless charity. You can always ask your GP or social worker if you have one. Now if they had a booze bank, I'd be first in the queue for booze bank vouchers.'

'Now that's not a bad shout. It would save all these shops from having their display cabinets decorated, eh Tom.'

That night we found ourselves in the local graveyard, one of Tom's favourite haunts. At least in there we wouldn't be bothered by anyone. It felt odd, lying on a bench surrounded by gravestones, but Tom was right, we both had a peaceful night's sleep. The week went by quickly. We spent a night in the hospital bus shelter again and were treated to another free cuppa around five in the morning. It was now Friday morning. There was still a chill in the air, but the sun was soon up in the sky and shining. The first sign that summer had arrived. It was time to get that great, all year round, tramp tan, well, only on your face. The same tan you'd come back off exercise with or from some far off shithole. We walked around for a while, so Wolfgang could do his business and exercise, then headed for Angie's Place for our weekly free cuppa and biscuits. I usually let Tom take the lead, but this time he'd forgotten the way and he seemed to be shuffling along instead of walking. He'd started doing that a lot recently.

'What's up Tom, lost your bearings?'
'Where are we going Andy?' He looked confused.
'Angie's Place Tom. It's Friday remember.'
'I know it's Friday,' he replied, sounding defensive.

Angie greeted us like long lost friends, as she did each time we went there. Sitting there, sipping our brew, I noticed Tom was looking frail. He'd lost a lot of weight since I first met him. It was a good job summer was here. I don't think Tom could last another winter without some proper care. I mentioned to him about seeing the doctor again. This time, it didn't piss him off because he'd forgotten about the last time I asked him.

'Tom, why don't you register with a doctor, or nip into a walk-in centre and sort that cough out?'
'Don't you worry about me son; I'll be ok. Thanks for your concern though.'
'There you go Tom, you've got mail,' said Angie, as

she placed a letter on the table, it was recorded delivery. Tom picked it up and quickly and put it in his pocket.

'Somebody you know, Tom?' I asked.

'Mind your own bloody business,' he replied.

'Now, now, Tom, no need for that language, I thought you two were friends.' Angie admonished him.

'We are friends aren't we Tom?' I said, while looking and smiling at him as I stirred my tea.

Tom was angry; he hated anyone asking questions. I got the feeling he was a little confused as well. 'So, you're not going to tell me who it's from then?' I said.

I found out later, that Tom had asked Angie if he could use her place as a forwarding address. I didn't ask him again. We moved on to another subject. Now it was Tom's turn to have a dig at me. I suppose every relationship has its ups and downs.

'So, when are you going to get yourself sorted Andy?' asked Tom. You shouldn't be on the streets now. Go and get yourself a place to stay, a job, and a girlfriend. It's not healthy out here for a young lad like you.'

'Are you trying to get rid of me Tom?'

'Yes,' he said with a smile, now I was getting the old Tom back again.

'Sorry Tom, I'm not quite ready yet, maybe in a few months. And if I find a place you can come and stay there with me. Would you do that?'

I knew what the answer would be; he just smiled, cradling his cup of sugary tea and said nothing. He was a stubborn old bugger, but I was there for him, I had his back. I had a reason to stay on the streets. It was this old fool. Even though he'd not admit it, he needed me. I made my mind up there and then that I would stay with him until I got him off the streets and in care.

'By the way boys, I will be closed next month for three weeks. I'm off on my holidays,' called out Angie, from behind the counter.

'Where are you going? Anywhere nice Angie?' I asked.

'I'm going to stay at my sister's place, down in Devon. I haven't seen her in years.'

'We could do with a holiday. Anywhere would do me. What about you Tom?'

'Bournemouth,' replied Tom. 'I'd like to go to Bournemouth.'

'Bournemouth... Why Bournemouth? I was thinking somewhere a little closer, like Blackpool or Skegness. We could doss on the beach.'

'Bournemouth,' said Tom again 'I'll toss you for it.'

'You're on.' I said.

Tom took out a coin from his coat and prepared to toss it.

'Heads we go to Bournemouth, tails Skegness,' he said.

'I don't believe I'm doing this, tails,' I replied.

Tom tossed the coin. It was heads; it had to be didn't it.

'So, when do we leave for Bournemouth, Andy?' Tom gave me a triumphant look.

'Sorry boys, I open in five minutes. It's time for you to leave,' Angie said, walking over to our table, carrying her usual can of air freshener.

After fuelling up at Angie's place we headed off downtown to our usual begging spots to try out new methods. Tom hadn't finished teaching me yet. **My favourite was the slot monkey.** Sitting outside arcades or the bookies were great places to beg, depending who you begged from. If some lucky punter has just walked out after winning a shed load of money, they'll be more likely to part with a few quid. They feel great, a king for a day. "I know, why don't I give that homeless person a fiver. What the hell, I can afford it." That was their good deed for the day. But if you get it wrong and ask them on a bad day, you might get a kick in the ribs for your troubles or worse. So, arcades are a bit of a gamble! Another one is **cash point stalker.** Sit yourself down close to a cash point machine, preferably down wind. Your **poor hygiene will make them uncomfortable.** When you've just sat and watched them draw out their wages, pop the question, "you haven't got a few quid to spare have you?" They can't say no can they, as they stand there, busily shoving twenty quid notes in their pockets? Sometimes you get lucky.

It was now one o'clock, the busiest time of the day, when everyone is on their lunch break. We'd already made a few quid and Wolfgang was getting restless, he wanted his biscuits. We decided to give it another twenty minutes and then we'd be off.

'What about those **aluminium cans,** the bins are full of them, isn't there any money in that anymore? I asked.

'Nah,' said Tom. You'd have to pick up thousands of them just to make a few pence. It's not worth it. But it is worth a go every now and then, for other reasons. If you pour the dregs out of every can you pick up into a single can, you can stop and refresh yourself from time to time.'

Took me a while that one, before I realised he was

taking the piss. Later that afternoon, a new face appeared on the street. I could recognise most of the homeless people by now but this guy looked unfamiliar, until I got up close. I was sure I knew him from somewhere. Tom said he'd seen him a few times a while back. Sat against the wall, dressed up in military gear from head to toe, he resembled an explosion in an army surplus shop. In front of him lay a beret, which was full of money. It's amazing what a flash of camouflage and a sign saying, ARMY VETERAN WITH PTSD PLEASE HELP can do to increase your chances of making a few quid. I walked over to introduce myself.

'I haven't seen you around here before,' I said.

'I'm not in your spot, am I?' the newcomer replied, sounding nervous.

'No mate, you go ahead.' I just had to ask him what unit he was in. 'So, you're a vet I see.'

'That's right. I was with 3 Para...' Then a barrage of bullshit followed. It was like the bloke was blowing into a fucking huge trumpet, all for himself. Before he said anything else, I jumped in.

'Of course you were mate,' I said.

Then I realised why he looked familiar. I couldn't believe it, I knew this guy, and we'd been in training together. 'Dropping out of basic does not make you a veteran with PTSD fella. Ex Para my arse,' I said. My blood was boiling, I felt like punching him.

Suddenly, he gathered his stuff, got up and marched off.

'Yes, you'd better fuck off too. Stealing people's valour, you wanker.'

Tom came wandering over, looking concerned.

'Steady on Andy, what the hell did you say to him?'

'He said he was with 3 Para. I recognised him, his name's Dave Coates, he joined up the same time as me. PTSD for fucks sake, what from, too many press-ups? He was only in a few weeks before he was released. He couldn't handle it. He's an A1, standard, gold plated, turbo Pinocchio. No wonder that genuine people suffering with PTSD don't get a fair deal. With people like him around, they don't stand a chance. What's the betting, as soon as he's out of sight, he'll be jumping in his twenty grand car that he's parked around the corner, and heading for the next town, for more of the same, before he heads home to mummy. The guy is a scam artist.'

Tom could see I was mad and he didn't waste any time trying to calm me down.

'You wanted to know what I did in the military didn't you? I was a Commodore you know.'

'Really,' I said, wondering if the brick wall was finally coming down.

'Yeah, Until Lionel Richie left, and then it all went tits up. Come on, let's move on.'

That's the thing with Tom; he has to make a joke out of every situation.

CHAPTER 10

A few more days went by without much happening. We'd managed to find a nice quiet spot to hang out, just outside town. Behind a row of shops, we found two old skips, one full of old rubble, and the other empty, apart from a load of bubble wrap. It looked like they belonged to a nearby abandoned building project, the perfect hideaway. Once we'd stocked up on supplies, we decided this was going to be our home for the weekend. We managed to drag a large piece of polythene over the empty skip to waterproof it, and then secured it with bricks before we climbed in. The bubble wrap sent Wolfgang mental. At first, he just kept popping the bubbles with his teeth. After a while he stopped. The novelty had worn off, just in time, it was a good job it did, our makeshift mattress was slowly deflating. Skips weren't usually our style, but it was getting warmer, and warmer weather brings out more rough sleepers, which meant most places around town were taken. This place was undiscovered, for now anyway. As long as we kept a look out for the local kids who had a habit of setting fire to skips, we'd be ok. And anyway, we always had Wolfgang, our intruder alarm. Tom and I talked for ages about stupid stuff. I did notice though that he was starting to drink more now. Which wasn't much fun for me, unless I joined in, which I did quite often. Then the conversation soon turned from stupid stuff, to utter bollocks. Tom was the expert in that line of conversation.

'You know what Andy, I'm sick of these kerb-crawling, professional business women, who patrol the streets late at night, looking for dirty old tramps and poor homeless men to have sex with. It's bloody disgusting.'

'What the fuck are you going on about Tom, are you winding me up again?' You've lost the plot. I might have to put you out of your misery soon, I'm not looking forward to doing it, but it's the kindest thing to do. You've had a good innings.'

'I see them almost every night. They've tried to get me inside their BMW or Jag loads of times. There's no fucking way I'm stepping foot in those women's cars, just so they can drive me into the middle of nowhere and have their wicked way with me. Then they have the neck to bung me a fifty quid note and throw me back onto the street like a piece of meat.'

'Tom, I think you need to stop drinking.'

'It would be good though, wouldn't it? if that happened.'

'In your dreams, have you ever met any homeless women on your travels Tom?'

'One or two, I'm useless with women. I remember once I asked this homeless woman if I could take her home and she smiled and said yes. I couldn't believe my luck. The look on her face soon changed though, when I walked off with her cardboard box.'

That made me laugh! I spat my lager all over the place. That's the thing with Tom; he's got a funny story for every situation.

'Watch it, I've just bought this suit. For fuck's sake.' Tom was on form tonight. 'Dating a woman who is homeless does have its advantages though. For one, it's easier to get them to stay over, and two, you can drop them off anywhere.'

'That's enough now Tom, I'm knackered, I need my sleep.'
'I bet they are absolutely filthy in bed.'
'Go to sleep now, you're pissed.'

On the second night, around one o'clock, I was suddenly woken by Wolfgang. He didn't bark, he just shot up into a sitting position and tilted his head, as though he was listening to something. I thought I was back in the army for a moment. It took me a while to get my bearings. I wondered where I was, then I realised I was lying in a skip with and old tramp and his dog. Tom was still fast asleep.

'What is it Wolfgang?' I whispered.

Then I heard noises, someone or something was rummaging around outside. I hoped it wasn't the local kids looking for something to set fire to. I peered through the gap between the skip and the plastic. I could see two figures about forty yards away. They looked like they were attempting to break into one of the shops. I don't know why, call it instinct; I just had to take a closer look, a sort of listening patrol. As I got closer my suspicions were right, one of them was in the process of climbing out of the window of one of the shops, the other one was helping him, they had two black holdalls full of something. I found out later the bags were full of mobile phones. I thought for a moment. Shall I challenge them or crawl back into my temporary accommodation? It was a catch twenty-two situation. If I didn't do anything then come the morning we'd probably get the blame for the robbery. If I did, I could take a bit of a beating. All sorts of thoughts were in my head. Why should I care? Too late, Wolfgang had made my mind up for me because he began to bark loudly. A torch was shone in my direction, then directly in my face, which totally destroyed any night vision I had. The one on the ground charged towards me and started to grapple with me.

'Who the fuck are you?' he asked.

'Easy lad, I'm just a homeless guy, I don't want any trouble,' I replied.

'Well, you've got it mate,' said the other one, who had come over to support his partner in crime.

The one who had grappled with me, started to punch out and caught me a few times. I tried to defend myself but I couldn't do a thing. He was getting the better of me. I managed to pull off his balaclava during the struggle and then the other one joined in. Wolfgang did his best to help by pulling at their trousers, trying to pull them off me. It was then that I was struck with something and fell to the ground. They dropped what they were carrying and fled. Tom slept through the whole episode. Thinking about it, it was probably a good thing he did. He was in no fit state to be fighting anybody.

I woke up on a hospital ward, with a copper looking down at me.

'I just want to ask you a few questions' he said. 'You're a bit of a hero son because of the way you tackled those two thugs.' A nurse joined the policemen and began tidying my bedding.

It took me a while to come to my senses. The last thing I remembered was tackling the two burglars at the back of the shops. How the hell did I end up in here?

'Will someone tell me what's going on?' I asked.

'You are in hospital; you were bought in during the

early hours of yesterday morning. You sustained a nasty blow to the head, which required twelve stitches. Because you've sustained a head injury, we need to keep you in for a few days' answered the nurse.

'Don't worry, you'll be glad to know we've got them and they're both in custody. Thanks to you pulling the balaclava off one of them, we were able to ID him on the CCTV, and then the other one owned up. Would you mind answering a few questions?' said the policeman.

'I'm afraid that won't be possible officer, not today, come back tomorrow,' said the nurse.

'But it's only a few questions. It should only take a few minutes.' He persisted.

I started to ask questions of my own. 'Where are Tom and Wolfgang, are they alright?'

'Who?' The policeman looked confused.

'I'm sorry,' the nurse continued, 'this patient is badly concussed. He needs rest and is in no fit state to be answering questions constable.'

The nurse and the policeman walked away together. I must have drifted back to sleep for a while. I woke up a few hours later, to find Tom sitting in a seat beside my bed. I knew it was Tom without even opening my eyes, I could ID that smell anywhere on the planet. It was so strong.

'You're awake,' he said.

'Can you tell me what's happening,' I asked, hoping to get a straight answer.

'You're in hospital, about to go down for a full lobotomy! Why didn't you wake me up? I thought we were buddies, we could have easily taken them together,' Tom said, sounding rather annoyed.

'What happened? All I remember was being hit on the head with something.'

'The copper told me you got hit with a torch. They left it behind. To be fair to the coppers, they were on the scene in seconds. The intruder alarm went off and that's what woke me up.'

I was in a room with three other people who were starting to notice the smell. One of them must have pressed their buzzer and complained because it wasn't long before Tom was approached by one of the female nursing assistants.

'How did you get in here? Visiting time is not until two o'clock,' she said, frowning.

'It's ok, I had a word with the sister,' Tom replied.

The nursing assistant didn't believe him and went off looking for the sister. I knew it wouldn't be long before they found out the truth. There was no way anyone would let Tom in the hospital willingly.

'She's on to you Tom. How did you get in here?' I asked.

'I sneaked past the security. It took me three attempts to get in this place to see you. I fooled them though. I took the lift to the geriatric ward on the top floor, and then took the lift back down again. I've probably only got a few more minutes before they track me down on the CCTV.'

'Where's Wolfgang?' I was worried he may have been injured as well.

'He's at Angie's. She's looking after him, he's ok. I had to take him to the vet this morning because he swallowed too much of that bloody bubble wrap, he keeps popping all the time. The vet said he'd be ok in a few days. I've got to wait until it's gone through his system. Here, I nearly forgot, I got you these.'

Tom put his hand in his pocket and pulled out a bunch of grapes and popped one in his mouth.

'Mmm, these are nice, taste one.' He pushed the grapes towards me.

'Where did you get those from?' I asked, pulling a few from the bunch.

'Where do you think I got them from? It's amazing what you find in these hospital bins... I bought them you idiot. Listen Andy, we've got a problem, well you have anyway.'

'What do you mean?'

'Do you want the good news or the bad news?'

'Just tell me.'

'The good news is, you're the local hero. Look at this.'

He passed me the newspaper, the headlines read... HAVE A GO HOMELESS HERO FIGHTS ROBBERS.

'How did they get my mug shot?'

'The whole incident was caught on CCTV, so according to the paper, it says you put up a good fight until you got pole axed by that metal torch. You've even made the regional news on TV; people love a hero. You're famous Andy, everyone's talking about you out on the street, that's where the problem is, so now for the bad news. The two scum bags you tackled were a couple of the Hardman brothers, Johnny and Phil.'

'Who are the Hardman's?'

'They are the sons of Ronny Hardman. He's still doing time for attempted murder. They are fucking nut cases mate.' Replied Tom.

'So, why are you telling me?'

'All I can say is that you're in the right place, because this is where you'll end up when the rest of their family catch up with you. In other words, we need to get the hell out of Derby. At least until it all blows over,' explained Tom.

Just then, I spotted the nursing assistant, accompanied by two burly security guards, walking up the ward towards us. Tom's visit was about to come to an abrupt end.

'Look out Tom, here they come,' I warned him.

'Come on you, you know you shouldn't be in here, this is a hospital and a tramp free zone,' one of the security guards said.

'And where's the sign that says that?' Tom was on form.

'If I remember rightly, aren't you the guy responsible for stealing the alcohol hand gel? Come on; let's have you out. My God you stink.' The guard had grabbed hold of Tom's arm.

'I am not touching him,' said the other guard.

'Get your hands off me!' Tom demanded.

'If he's going, I'm going. Where's my clothes?' I said

'No, you stay where you are sir.' the nursing assistant tried to prevent me getting out of bed.

'I'm a tramp, the same as him, if he's not welcome, then neither am I,' I said to her.

'Mister Jones, get back in bed,' she pleaded.

The two guards started to manhandle Tom off the ward. He wasn't going quietly.

'Get off me, you wankers!'

I started to get dressed. I was determined to leave with Tom.

'Mister Jones, you need to stay here until the doctor has seen you tomorrow.'

'Sorry mate, got to go. I'll be ok. I've had worse. Give the bed to someone that needs it. I need to be with my friend, he needs me more.'

I caught up with Tom and his escort at the exit.

'Right, next time we see you here, we'll call the police,' one of the guards warned him.

'I could sue you two. Did you see how they treated me? It's all on camera you know.'

'Come on Tom, let's go.' I guided Tom off the hospital grounds and we headed for Angie's, to pick up Wolfgang.

'You didn't have to leave Andy. You should have stayed in hospital.'

'I'm just heeding your warning that's all. What was it you said? "Don't outstay your welcome in a hospital... it can be a downward cycle...a revolving door" You see I did take in some of the things you taught me. So where are we going? You said we needed to get out of Derby. We don't have to decide today do we?'

'There's no time like the present,' Tom said.

Tom looked nervous and didn't stop looking around. The Hardman's were a petty crime gang. A group of ten or more individuals, most of them related, who liked to think they ruled the local estates. To be really honest, I wasn't that worried, but Tom was. If it meant us getting out of Derby to pastures new, I'd go with it. We needed a change. I'd had enough of Derby. We arrived at Angie's and Wolfgang did his usual thing when he saw Tom and started to roll around on the floor with joy.

'You were very brave, I read all about it in the paper', Angie informed me. 'It's all over the front cover you know.'

'I wasn't brave at all. To be honest, I can't remember

much about it.'

'Here, they let you out of the hospital early, didn't they? It only happened the other night.' Angie sounded concerned.

'No, they said I could go home. Who wants a smelly tramp on the ward anyway?'

'Go home? Where is home, Andy?' Tom asked, laughing.

'Sit down, I'll make you both a drink,' Angie said.

'But Angie, it's not Friday morning, you're breaking your own rules,' I reminded her.

'It's not every day I get a real hero in my cafe. You should get a reward for what you did young man.'

'I think she's taken a shine to you Andy,' Tom said, out of earshot.

'What was that Tom?' Angie asked.

'I said we are thinking of moving on Angie,' Tom answered.

'Where to love? Is this the little holiday you were talking about?' Angie replied.

'Bournemouth, what do you think Tom? You won that bet remember.'

Tom didn't answer me. He was too busy staring out of the window. Looking out for unwanted guests. He was obviously worried about me being tracked down by the local thugs.

'Did you hear me Tom? Are we going to Bournemouth?' I asked.

'Yes,' he said, looking a little confused.

'Are you alright Tom?' I was worried because these looks of confusion were happening more often.

'Yes, I just came over a little dizzy, that's all, must be the withdrawal symptoms, I haven't had a drink today,' he replied.

'Oh, you'll love it there. How are you are going to get there may I ask?' Angie loved being the organiser.

'That's the problem, we're a little short on funds, but we'll find a way. Tom's always got something up his sleeve, haven't you mate?'

'It's ok, we've got the money,' Tom answered.

'Have we, since when?' I was surprised by his reply.

Tom pulled out a bundle of notes from his hat. There looked to be at least two or three hundred pounds in his hand.

'Wow, you kept that quiet.' I wondered how long he'd had the money for and where it came from.

'I only received it the other day.' Said Tom.

Before I could ask any more questions, Angie took command.

'Right then, when are you thinking of going?'

'Today hopefully,' I replied.

'So quickly?' Angie sounded surprised.

'No time like the present,' Tom said.

Angie began using her phone to make some enquiries. I got the feeling she also wanted us to get out of Derby. She knew the gang well and knew there'd be reprisals. Angie knew everybody.

'You're in luck, there's a bus leaving at twelve minutes past seven tonight.'

'Sounds good to me,' Tom agreed.

'Right, if you two are serious about going to Bournemouth, you'd better get yourself sorted, there's no way they'll let you on a bus in that state. Look at you both,' she said.

It wasn't long before we were down the local charity shops looking for new clothes, with Angie's help. She had surprised me by closing the café to come with us. We grabbed anything that fitted us. Again, Tom wasn't happy, but we came to an arrangement. We agreed to wear the new clothes just for the journey. As soon as we got to Bournemouth, our tramp clothes would be back on. When we arrived back at Angie's, she sent us straight up to her flat above the cafe for a shower. Tom wasn't too pleased about that either, but it had to be done. Later that afternoon, we stood in Angie's café looking well smart, clean shaven and wearing our new clothes, but Tom still wouldn't part with that stupid hat.

'Just look at you both!' Exclaimed Angie. 'No one would have guessed you were both homeless a few hours ago. You've both been transformed and what a pair of handsome chaps you both are.'

Angie was a little tearful and it wasn't just the shock of seeing us like this. Angie had known Tom for a very long time, and I think she knew deep down, she probably wouldn't see Tom again. He always said to her "Once I move on, I never return to the same place."

'It's time to go lads. You'll miss your bus. Keep in touch won't you?' she asked.

We both gave her a big hug and it was an emotional goodbye. Angie started to cry and Tom tried his hardest to hold back the tears as we walked away, but a stray tear escaped and rolled down his cheek. We walked down the road carrying our old clothes in black bin liners. We turned once, to wave at Angie, but she had already gone inside. I think it was all a little too much for her.

'I've only had three real friends you know. You, Angie and Wolfgang,' said Tom tearfully.

'You're wrong Tom. What about the two thousand fleas that you're carrying in that black bag of yours,' I said jokingly.

CHAPTER 11

The bus station was about a mile away. Tom shuffled along slowly. It was becoming obvious the long hard winter had taken its toll on him. Hopefully, the change of scene would do him good. I'd decided that once we got there, I'd get him in to see a doctor, even if I had to drag him there.

'Well, it's now or never Tom, are you sure you want to do this?'

'Yes,' he said. 'I've never been to the seaside you know.'

'What? You're winding me up aren't you, of course you've been to the seaside you silly old bugger.'

'I'm telling you. I've never seen the seaside.'

I just ignored him. His memory was failing, yet another reason why I had to get him seen by a doctor. On the way to the bus station, we passed all the places that had provided us with shelter, the hostel, the church, the sex shop doorway, the pavilion and the bus shelters. The hospital where the security officers had given us free drinks and not forgetting the many bins that had provided us with meals, as a last resort. I know it sounds stupid, but those places were part of our home, more so for Tom, than me. Once at the bus station, Tom took out a bundle of money, enough to pay for our tickets, including Wolfgang's.

'I really appreciate you paying for my ticket Tom. I'll make sure you get the money back, as soon as...'

'Shut up you idiot.' Snapped Tom. 'I'd just waste it on booze anyway. Speaking of booze...'

We had around twenty-five minutes before the bus arrived. So, the decision was made that I'd head for the bus station café to get the brews in, while Tom headed across the road to the supermarket to buy refreshments for the journey. We arranged to meet back at the bus station in ten minutes. I entered the café with Wolfgang and walked up to the counter, carrying our bags of clothes.

'Two teas please,' I said to the middle-aged woman behind the counter.

'Going far?' she asked.

'Yes, me and my friend are off to Bournemouth for a few weeks.'

'The weather is supposed to be lovely down there for the next few days,' she informed me.

'Oh, that's good.' A little bit of sun would do Tom the world of good I thought.

'Quarter past seven bus then?' she asked.

'What? Oh yes, that's right.'

'It's the number 405,' she continued.

'Cheers,' I replied. The woman had obviously worked at the café for a long time, for her to know the bus timetables and numbers.

'I know you. You're that homeless guy who stopped those robbers. Your picture is in the papers,' she said.

Not another one I thought. She then passed me the teas.

'I'm not homeless, I'm a tramp,' I told her.

'Ok, if you say so. Here don't tell anyone...you have those teas on the house...go on, and well done. It's about time someone taught those scum bags a lesson. They think they can go around robbing places and bullying folk, well, I'm not scared of them,' she replied.

While we were talking away, two youths entered the café and sat down near the door. I didn't really take any notice of them. I sat down and started to drink my tea, thinking about the prospect of holidaying in sunny Bournemouth. The change will be good for the both of us. The two youths were now staring at me and smiling. I avoided eye contact, whoever they might be; I didn't want to get into some sort of confrontation, which was that last thing I needed. I was starting to worry. I looked up at the café clock, it was nearly five past seven and our bus would be leaving soon. Where the hell was Tom? It had been fifteen minutes since Tom headed off to the shop. It was only over the road, what was taking him so long? I got up to leave, to go and search for him.

'Going somewhere pal, or running away?' said one of the two youths. They were now standing in front of the door, one behind the other.

'Look, I don't know who the fuck you both are, but I've got a bus to catch.'

'You ain't going anywhere mate, it's payback time. Do you know the Hardman's?'

'Oh, that's what this is all about is it? Listen lads, like I said, I don't want any trouble, ok.'

The nearest one to me walked towards me in an aggressive manner, while the other stood by the door. The woman that had served me earlier moved out from behind the counter and started to shout.

'You both need to leave right now, or I'm calling the police, come on, out!' she shouted.

They took no notice and just laughed. The youth in

front of me threw a punch, but I saw it coming and ducked. I then threw a punch back, which connected with his jaw and knocked him clean out, he fell to the floor. His buddy pushed the café assistant out of the way as he went to the aid of his mate, only to be hit on the back of the head with a large pan. The impact sounded like a sound effect from a Tom and Jerry cartoon. He struggled back to his feet and went to lash out at her. Before he knew it, I was all over him. I'd grabbed him round the neck and dragged him to the floor, tightly gripping his neck until he'd stopped moving. Wolfgang just sat there and watched the whole thing. He must have thought, 'Not again, I'm steering clear of this one.'

That's when Tom walked in. I could see him taking in the scene before him.

'What the bloody hell is going on? I leave you alone for fifteen minutes and look what happens.'

I released the lad on the floor. I'd either squeezed his neck a little too hard, or the café assistant's pan had knocked him out. His friend was beginning to come round.

'I don't want to rush you Andy but our bus is outside and we need to go.'

'Go on,' said the assistant, 'catch the bus, don't worry, I've got this under control, the police are on their way, it's all on CCTV. If you weren't famous already, you're famous now, and thanks. These two have been coming in here abusing my staff for months. It's about time someone put them in their place.'

She put her hand up for a high five and I obliged. We grabbed our gear, including Wolfgang, and left to board the bus. It was more or less empty, so we headed for the back seat. It was going to be a long journey, so hopefully we could stretch out. Five minutes later, the bus left the station, just as the police arrived.

'What was all that about? It was the Hardman's wasn't it? I knew they'd be on the warpath. I told you, didn't I.'

'You did mate.'

'I recognised one of them. He's done time for stabbing someone, he's a Nutter.'

'Thanks for that. Now you tell me! Well, we're out of here now, Tom.'

'You're turning out to be a bit of a vigilante,' he said.

'All I did was protect myself.'

'Protect yourself? You knocked one out and near strangled the other one.'

'No, it was just a chokehold. I was merely restraining his head to stop him from hurting himself. He felt so safe and secure he went to sleep.... and anyway, I had help.'

'Your honour...is that what you're going to say in court?'

'Fuck off Tom, stop winding me up.'

Tom sat near the window, on the driver's side, and I was sat next to him at first. There were only four other people on the bus, two lads sitting a few rows ahead of us, and sitting opposite them there were two young girls, who looked around sixteen or seventeen years old. Once the bus had pulled away, we sat Wolfgang between us. We had a six-hour journey before we arrived in Bournemouth. The bus hadn't even left the station before Tom decided to open his first can of lager.

'Steady on Tom, they've got to last you six hours.'

'We're off on our holiday Andy so I'm just getting in the holiday mood. Don't worry about me. After a few cans of this I'll be asleep for most of the journey. Look, we've got the whole back seat to ourselves.'

'That's why I chose these seats. You see, I was thinking of you Tom.'

He offered me a can and I gladly took it. He was right, it was getting dark, six hours was a long time to be staring out of the window at your own reflection. The bus was well on its way. As we headed down the A38 towards Birmingham, it felt good. I was glad to get out of Derby for new surroundings. I wondered what Bournemouth would bring. We didn't waste any time sorting out the sleeping arrangements. We were both spread out on the back seat, fast off. I woke up a few times when the bus stopped to let on more passengers. I looked over at Tom and he was out of it. The bus was now half full. We'd been travelling for nearly four hours when voices, coming from the seats a few rows in front of us, woke me up.

'Fucking hell, can you smell that?'

'Yes, what is it?'

'It's that old man lying on the back seat, he stinks of piss.'

I sat up. I'd been listening to these two young lads trying to chat up the young girls for a while. But now they were making the two young girls laugh, at Tom's expense and I wasn't having it.

'What was that, what did you say about my mate?'

I took them by surprise. They didn't say anything; they just looked straight-ahead, red faced. The girls just giggled away. They were right though. The smell of urine was strong. I needed to wake him up and sort him out.

'Tom, Tom, wake up mate.'
'I'm awake. What is it?'
'Do you need the toilet?'
'Yes, but I'll be alright, I can wait till we stop again.'
'There's a toilet on the bus, Tom.'
'A toilet on a bus... Who ever heard of a toilet on a bus?'
'Come on Tom, how many lagers have you had?' I looked in the bag and saw it was empty. He'd drunk the lot. All five cans.

Then I got a whiff of something much worse. The smell travelled up the bus and now everyone was looking in our direction.

'Do you know him? Has he shit, himself? He has hasn't he?' said one of the lads.

Tom looked confused as I lifted him upright.

'Tom, have you messed yourself mate?'
'No, I don't think so. It must be Wolfgang. It's definitely not me,' he replied.

Tom soon realised he was the centre of attention. Everyone was looking at him.

'What the fuck are they all looking at?' Tom asked in a raised voice.

'That's disgusting mate. Sort yourself out!' one of the youths shouted.

'Get him off the bus,' said multiple voices.
'Give the guy a break will you,' I pleaded.

Most of the people who sat near us got up and moved down to the front of the bus.

'It's not Wolfgang, is it Tom?' Wolfgang was fast asleep, oblivious to the whole situation.

'Sorry Andy.' Tom started to cry.

'What are you crying for mate, don't cry. We'll get it sorted, come on.'

I guided him to the toilet. Once inside I helped him clean himself up, it took ages. All he kept saying was sorry. I was glad Angie had made us buy more than one set of clothes at the charity shop.

'It's ok Tom, shit happens,' I said. We both started to laugh. 'We've all done it after a night on the piss,' I said. I just thought I'd say that to reassure him.

After thirty minutes, we were all good to go. We emerged from the toilet and took up our seats again, although Tom couldn't sit by the window now because the seat was wet. There was still a faint smell in the air, but not as bad. The air conditioning had done its job. Tom sat quietly with Wolfgang, who was now sitting in his lap.

'I couldn't help it you know, it wasn't because of the lager. I just couldn't stop myself, it's happening more often now,' he confessed.

'So, you've had this problem for a while. Why didn't you tell me Tom? I told you to see a doctor. Didn't I?'

'I need to tell you something Andy.'

Our conversation was cut short by the bus suddenly pulling up at the side of the road. The driver got up out of his seat and walked down the bus towards us.

'Sorry, but I'm afraid I'm going to have to ask you both to get off the bus.'

'Why, what have we done?' Tom asked.

'Look at you, you're drunk, look at all those empty cans and that's without what happened earlier, the bus stinks. The bus needs cleaning, I've got no choice but to head for the nearest depot and transfer all the passengers to another bus,' said the irate bus driver.

'I'm not going anywhere, I paid for my ticket, same as everyone else,' Tom said.

'Come on mate. Give us a break. The least you could do is drop us off at the next town. We're in the middle of nowhere here,' I pleaded.

'I'm sorry. I have to think of the safety of the other passengers. You have to get off the bus now, please, or I'll have to call the police.'

'Well, call the fucking police. I'm not bothered,' Tom said, getting more agitated by the minute.

'You were swearing at my passengers. Like I said, I have to think of their safety.'

I realised that we were wasting our time. There was no way the driver would drive the bus while we were still on it. I made a decision that I knew Tom wouldn't like it, but it was our only option.

'Come on Tom, let's get off,' I said, helping him up out of his seat.

We grabbed our things and walked slowly down the aisle, followed by Wolfgang. The other passengers on the bus didn't say a word; there was total silence. They just looked the other way and I couldn't blame them. We stood at the side of the road, watching our bus disappear into the distance.

'I hated that bus anyway,' Tom said, giving a two-fingered salute to the departing bus.

'Did you see the state of the toilet? It was bloody disgusting and there was lager cans everywhere, never again!' I replied.

'Same here, if I never see another bus it will be too soon,' Tom added.

I looked around but there were no road signs, just a few lights in the distance, in the place where we'd just come from. I hadn't a clue where we were.

'So, what now, where are we?' said Tom, 'we could be anywhere, we need to head south don't we, that's where Bournemouth is, isn't it?'

'Yep, you're right. I know what we'll do. We'll navigate our way using the stars,' I answered.

'What?' Tom looked at me as though I was a raving lunatic.

Although it was a little windy, it wasn't cold, which made a change. Looking up at the night sky, I looked for the constellations I recognised; luckily it was a clear night. There were no clouds or light pollution. Perfect. I could see the stars clearly.

'Right, first we need to find the Polaris Star, the North Star...' I said.

Tom stood there clueless, scratching his head. He was starting to sober up quickly.

'... And to do that we need to find 'The Plough', also known as the 'Big Dipper' to our American friends and the 'Saucepan' to others.'

'What's this, fucking 'Sky at Night?' you've lost it, Andy,' said Tom, shaking his head, unable to believe what I was saying.

'The Plough rotates anti clockwise around it,' I continued.

'The who?' Tom was looking more confused by the minute.

'There it is, the North Star. That means we need to head in the opposite direction, south,' I replied.

'You've lost me but if you say so.' Tom shrugged his shoulders.

'Grab your stuff Tom and follow me. We'll just keep walking until we find somewhere to doss for the night.'

We walked, in Tom's case, shuffled, along for the next hour. It must have been well past midnight before we both admitted we'd had enough. In the distance, we could just about make out the outlines of what looked like buildings, silhouetted on the skyline. There were no streetlights or house lights, which I thought was strange, but the houses were in our path, so we headed for them. We reached the buildings and discovered that it was a small village. We walked past what looked like the empty shells of houses, on both sides of the road. It was all very haunting. Before long, we were through the village and out the other side.

'Time to find a place to doss for the night Tom, I think.'

'Good and about time,' Tom answered. He was really struggling now.

We turned off the road and negotiated a barbed wire fence into some open ground, then over another fence, and yet another one. I wanted to get as far away from the road as possible. The further away from prying eyes the better, in my opinion. I looked back and saw that Tom had had enough. He'd flopped down to the ground, with Wolfgang.

'How far are we going Andy because I'm done,' he said, sounding breathless.

'We can doss here if you want, this bank will shield us from the wind.'

I joined Tom on the ground. Luckily it was a dry and fairly warm night, so there was no need to find shelter. We both sat in silence for a few minutes, glad of the rest. There were enough bits of dead wood around for us to get a small fire going. I looked across at Tom, by the light of the fire. Our late night trek had done him no favours, his face was drained of colour and he was still struggling to bring his breathing under control.

'Bloody hell, that was a bit of a tab wasn't it? You did well Tom, but how are you feeling?' I asked.

'I'm ok. Is that star still there?'

'I don't think it'll be going anywhere soon, Tom. I know this is a stupid question, but did you buy any food when you bought the booze or was it just a liquid diet you had in mind? I'm starving.'

'Of course, I did.'

'Brilliant, get it out then, I could eat a scabby cat.'

You should have seen the smile on my face when Tom produced a large cooked chicken. My mouth started to water at the prospect of eating it.

'Not for you though, it's for Wolfgang.' Tom informed me. 'Look what I've got Wolfie, a whole chicken, just for you. The dog started to get excited, wagging his tail whilst waiting for his meal, which Tom dangled above his head teasingly.

'So, what do we get then?' I asked, looking longingly at the chicken.

Tom pulled out two bags of cheese and onion crisps, and a can of lager that he must have hidden earlier. I looked at Wolfgang with envy.

'So, the dog gets a whole fucking chicken and we get crisps, plus I hate cheese and onion by the way.'

Just as I said that, Tom ripped off a leg and passed it to me. 'Here, now stop your moaning.'

We all tucked in. I was busy biting into the chicken leg but Tom's next statement stopped me in my tracks and I started to change colour.

'Mmm... not bad for chicken that's two days past its

use by date.'

'But you bought it this evening, didn't you?' I said, not believing that a shop would sell a chicken that far past its use by date.

'No, I found it in the supermarket bin,' replied Tom.

'For fucks sake Tom,' I said and passed it back to him.

'Well, I did tell you it was for Wolfgang.'

I spat out what was in my mouth and opened my crisps. Wolfgang was enjoying his chicken. It must have made a nice change from dog biscuits and scraps.

'Enjoying your last lager Tom?' I said, watching him knocking it back.

'I'm sure there'll be shops somewhere around here.' he replied between mouthfuls.

'Talking of lager, what happened on the bus Tom? Was it the lager that did it? You were about to tell me something before the driver came along, what was it?'

'Was I, I can't remember. It couldn't have been anything important, anyway, what did happen on the bus?'

'There you go again, bottling it up Tom. You can talk to me about anything you know.'

Tom didn't answer me; the poor sod looked confused. I think he genuinely couldn't remember. I knew now that there was something seriously wrong with him. We sat quietly for a while, with just the red glow from the small fire on our faces, and then Tom spoke.

'When was the last time you saw your mum and dad, Andy?'

'About a year ago,' I replied.

'That long, why?'

'We fell out. My dad has always been a straight talker. Always spoke his mind. He told me that Sally, my ex, was no good for me, way before I realised it myself. Well, you know how it is, so I stuck with my wife for better or for worse and all that. All he said was, "Your bed son, you made it, now lay in it."'

'He was right then,' Tom said.

'Yep, he sure was.'

'So, I'm guessing you're too proud, just like your dad, to go and tell him he was right.'

'He'd love that. Yes, I can just see him now, standing on the doorstep saying, "I told you so." No, I just don't want to burden them with my shit, that's all.'

'And what about your mum?'

'My mum just agrees with whatever my dad says but I love her to bits though. I can hear her saying now, "Go and ask your dad" whenever I asked her a question. Unless I was asking her "What's for dinner Mum?" and then her usual replies were "Shit with sugar on" or "bread and pull it." She's a very old fashioned woman, my mum.'

'You need to go and see them, they won't be around forever you know.'

'I will one day, when I've sorted myself out.' I changed the subject.

Talking about my mum and dad had made me feel sad. I wish I could turn back time, but that wasn't an option.

Wolfgang had finished his feast and was fast asleep, snuggled up close to Tom.

'Look at him, not care in the world. I wish life was that simple sometimes,' said Tom, sighing.

'This is like being back in the mob, Tom. Do you reckon we're safe here?'

'Safe, what from?' he asked.

'The enemy,' I replied. 'What time is it now? I'd say it must be gone midnight. I'll tell you what, you can do the twelve till two stag and I'll do the two till four, don't forget to stand to at 05.45 hours.'

I went on talking to myself for a few minutes, pretending I was back in the army. I could tell Tom wasn't impressed, on account of his loud snoring, in sync with Wolfgang. It was time to join them. Today had been an eventful day.

CHAPTER 12

I was awoken in the morning by the faint sound of tracked vehicles in the distance. They must be farm vehicles I thought. I stood up to see if I could spot them. They were too far away. Then the noise stopped and bird song took over. Tom was still sound off, lying next to Wolfgang and the discarded chicken bones from his meal the previous night. The fire was still smouldering and a half empty whisky bottle lay nearby him. No wonder he fell asleep so quickly. The sneaky fucker! I thought.

I wandered off to see if I could get my bearings. The place looked familiar to me for some reason. I walked about fifty yards up the side of the bank, then something that was lying on the ground, caught my eye. It was some sort of yellowish tin disc. Then everything fell into place because written on the can were the words 'Processed Cheese' Old compo rations and tracked vehicles. This was a training area. Wandering further down the bank I saw the backs of several large signs, they were next to the barbed wire fence that we'd climb over last night. Oh shit! I read the words on one of the signs and my worst fears had been realised.

WARNING TO THE PUBLIC

DO NOT ENTER

DANGER! UNEXPLODED BOMBS

DANGER! MILITARY DEBRIS

ON NO ACCOUNT SHOULD ANY OBJECT BE MOVED OR TOUCHED

We needed to get out of here! I rushed back, woke Tom and told him where we'd been sleeping. Tom was a little disorientated.

'What, slow down will you, what are you saying?'
'We need to be careful where we step, there's a warning sign down there saying unexploded bombs and military debris, for Christ sake don't pick anything up. But it was already too late for one of us. We heard a muffled explosion.
'What was that? Where's Wolfgang? Andy, was he with you? Tom said with a fearful look on his face.

We made our way over the bank. What was left of Wolfgang lay on the ground. Tom went running towards him. I shouted to Tom to watch out, but nothing would have stopped him. I stood back and I choked up as I looked down on the scene below me. Wolfgang was gone. He must have dug up a mortar shell or something. I'd taken us all into a fucking danger zone. It was me who'd decided to take the route from the road and now I felt like shit. Tom just knelt there in silence, rocking backwards and forwards, cradling what was left of the dog he loved so much. It was my fault. Tom looked over at me and he was crying like a baby.

'You and your North Star! Look what happened, you've killed my dog!'

I didn't know what to say. I was lost for words. All I knew was that we were both still in danger and that was my main concern now. The tracked vehicles got closer. There were four of them, all armoured personnel carriers. They stopped on the other side of the field, about two hundred metres away. While behind me, an army Land Rover had pulled up on the road. The driver got out and stood by the fence. I noticed the stripes on his arm and knew he was a sergeant.

'Stay where you are! You are in serious trouble sir!' Barked the sergeant, 'do you know you are not permitted in this area? It is extremely dangerous to civilians. What the hell are you doing here on Salisbury Plains? This place is dangerous, the signs are everywhere.'

'Salisbury Plains, are you kidding me?' I couldn't believe what he was saying.

I walked over towards him. I explained to him that we were homeless, and we were making our way to Bournemouth, until we were kicked off the bus in the middle of the night. The sergeant began to lower his tone.

'What happened over there, is that your friend?'

'He's just lost his dog. He must have dug something up.'

'I'm really sorry about that. I'll tell you what. I'll give you and your friend a few minutes and then I'll have to escort you off this area.'

He pointed out a safe track that we could use, once we were ready to leave.

'Thanks sergeant, I appreciate it.'

The sergeant walked back to his vehicle, and he was soon on his radio. I walked over to Tom. I had to get him away from danger.

'Come on Tom, we have to leave because the army is here.'

Tom ignored me, so I knelt down beside him and put my arm around him.

'He's gone mate,' I said.

'He never stood a chance, did he?' Tom said, with tears streaming down his face. 'I'm going to miss him Andy. I'm sorry I blamed you. It's not your fault.'

'That's all right, come on, let's get out of here,' I urged him.

'I want to bury him here,' he said, looking up at me.

'You can't bury him here mate, it's too dangerous.'

'I don't want anyone else to see him. I want to bury him here.' Tom was determined to get his own way.

I stood back whilst Tom placed Wolfgang in the hole that had been created by the explosion. He then covered him over with the loose earth. Tom said a few words, and then we walked back to the sergeant, who was waiting for us half way up the track.

'Tell me again, what the hell were you guys doing wandering around here?' the sergeant asked.

'It's a long story,' I said.

'I'm afraid you'll have to explain that to the police,' he replied.

He guided us away from the danger zone, to the safety of the road. Once at his vehicle, he picked up his radio again.

'Just stand there will you gents,' he instructed.

After he'd radioed in and told them we'd been safely recovered, he told us to jump on board.

'Is your friend ok?' he asked, when Tom didn't respond.

'He'll be all right, just give him a minute. He's not well.'

Tom stood about ten yards away, looking over at where Wolfgang was buried. Tears still streamed down his face. Wolfgang had been his constant companion for quite some time.

'I've dug holes in this place a few times,' I told the sergeant.

'You were in the army?'

'Yes. Infantry. My mate Tom was in the army as well.'

'So, you should have known this was a training area.'

'I didn't know until I heard the tracked vehicles and noticed the signs. We arrived here in the dark. Come to think of it, I should have realised last night, when we walked through that village. It's Imber, isn't it?'

'Yes, and that's out of bounds as well. So what unit was Tom in?' he asked.

I laughed and said 'the old bugger won't tell me, but he was definitely in the military. I've seen his ID card. He still carries it and looking at his regimental number, I'd guess he joined up in the early seventies. Be gentle with him sergeant, he's not well and he's very fragile, especially now.' I was feeling protective of my old friend.

We were waiting for clearance to move over the training area safely. I spent the next ten minutes explaining to the sergeant about our situation and how we had gotten here. He listened, intrigued.

'It sounds like you guys have had a hard time,' he said, sounding sympathetic.

Just then a message came over on the radio.

'Right gents, we've just had clearance, get yourselves on the back of the vehicle and we'll get you out of here.'

We both climbed on board and were driven away. I didn't speak to Tom. I felt he needed the space. We'd been travelling for around twenty minutes before Tom said anything.

'Where are we going?' he asked.

'The police station I think,' I replied.

I didn't mention it to him but there was that smell again. The same smell from the bus.

'You ok Tom?'

'I'm ok, Wolfgang's gone Andy. I can't bring him back can I?'

The vehicle turned left and into Battlesbury Barracks, near the town of Warminster. I knew this place. I'd been here before, only for a few nights. The Land Rover stopped outside the guardroom and the sergeant got out.

'Come on lads, de-bus, out you get. If you can just wait here for a second, I'll be back shortly.'

I could just about make out the sergeant explaining our situation to someone. Looking inside the guardroom, I could see the prison cells and the bed. The memories came flooding back. It's funny, I would have hated being a prisoner while I was in the army and have to have slept on one of those beds, but now, what I wouldn't give for a couple of nights kip on one of them! We looked well out of place. The regimental policeman was tasked to keep an eye on us. There were soldiers in uniform everywhere. We must have looked like a couple of vets that had gone AWOL years ago and had just been re-captured. The sergeant arrived back a few minutes later and he was smiling.

'Right lads, I've had a word with the **adjutant** and explained to him your situation and he's agreed, because you're both vets we're not going to inform the police. The good news is, we'd like you to be our guests, well at least until you've cleaned yourselves up and had a good meal.'

Tom and me looked at each other, we couldn't believe our luck.

'I don't know what to say. We'd be honoured, thank you,' I said.

'Don't worry, we'll look after you until you go on your way, it's the least we can do.'

We were then escorted to the sergeant's mess for the rest of that day. Where we were well looked after and given special treatment. We both had a shower and washed our dirty clothes. I was glad we had been given the use of the showers and laundry facilities as it gave me the opportunity to clean Tom up without embarrassing him. I remembered how upset he'd been on the bus. We were given as much food as we could eat. We watched TV and then we were taken to the sergeant's mess bar, to wait for our clothes to dry. It felt strange sitting in an army tracksuit again. They'd loaned us one each to wear, while our clothes dried.

'What are you drinking lads, it's on the house,' said the barman.

Tom's eyes lit up at the mention of drinks. We sat in the corner with our drinks. Tom didn't waste any time. His glass was almost empty before I'd taken a sip of my drink.

'Steady on Tom, it isn't going to run away you know,'

I said, hoping he'd slow down.

'You see, I told you there would be a pub round here.'

'Yep, you were right mate.'

The sergeant who had rescued us from the field soon joined us.

'Everything to your liking lads?' he asked.

'Yes thanks, you didn't have to go to all this trouble you know,' I answered.

'You speak for yourself,' Tom said jokingly, drinking the last dregs in his glass.

'Nonsense, one word to the adjutant and it was sorted. We look after our vets, you know. Right, what are you drinking? It's my round,' he said, as he stood up to go to the bar.

He soon returned with the lagers for Tom and me. He sat down with us for a while. I told him all about my army career and how I'd found myself out on the streets.

'What about you, old man, when did you become homeless?' he asked, turning to Tom.

'I'm not homeless, I'm a tramp and I choose to be on the streets. If you're asking me when I decided to become a tramp... I haven't got a clue. A long time ago.'

'I'm really sorry about your dog. I'll get my lads to put up a little plaque next time they're up that way. What was his name?'

It was then that I realised Tom wasn't right, he couldn't answer the sergeant. He just looked at me for help. It was now obvious that something was seriously wrong with him. Wolfgang had been the centre of his world so how could he have forgotten him so soon? I replied to the question that he couldn't answer.

'His name was Wolfgang. Bloody hell Tom, you've only had a few lagers.'

'Sorry, I need to use the toilet, you'll have to excuse me,' Tom said, as he stood up.

Tom headed for the toilet, helped along by the duty barman. 'Come on, old fella, it's this way.'

The sergeant and I looked down at where Tom had been sitting, the seat was wet and there was a puddle on the floor.

'He's not well, is he?' he asked.

'No, he hasn't been right for a while. He should be in hospital, but you try telling him that.'

'What unit was he in?'

'I've been asking him for months, but he won't say.'

'Or he's forgotten,' said the sergeant. 'Look, do you want me to have a word with the MO or we can get in touch with the local British Legion.'

'You are wasting your time. Tom has always said to me, "I've lived most of my life on the streets, I'll die on the streets."'

'But it might be something that can be sorted out,' the sergeant persisted.

'Look, I'll have a word, but I don't think he'll listen.'

Tom came shuffling across the room towards the table.

'Sorry about that, nature calls. Bloody hell this seat's wet? he said, glancing down.

'It's ok Tom, I spilt my drink, didn't I Andy? right I'll leave you guys to it,' said the sergeant as he headed towards the bar.

'Tom, we need to talk,' I told him.

'What is it Andy?'

'I think it's time to admit you need to see a doctor. The sergeant has very kindly offered to get the guys down the Med centre, to give you a quick check over if you want, how good is that.'

As usual, Tom gave me the silent treatment and carried on drinking his lager. I knew it would be an up hill battle to get him to admit he was ill and needed help.

'Andy, I don't want to see anyone. All I want to do now is go to the seaside that's all, please. I know you're concerned about me but I'll be ok.'

'Ok Tom, I'll let the sergeant know.'

I got up to talk to the sergeant, who was sat at the bar, but was stopped in my tracks by Tom.

'While you're up there, get them in will you? And don't look so sad, everything's going to be just fine, you'll see.'

At that moment, I felt like crying. Why couldn't he admit he was sick and in need of help? I vowed to myself to take him to see a doctor, once we had been to the seaside at Bournemouth. Maybe once he had seen the sea, he'd give in. I carried on across the room to the bar.

'So, did you manage to talk him round?' the sergeant asked.

'Not a chance, I told you he's a stubborn old bastard.'

'Proper old soldier isn't he. My old man was like that right to the end. Oh well, you've done your best fella. So where to next, didn't you say you were on your way to Bournemouth?'

'Yes, we'll have this last drink and we'll be on our

way. And thanks again for everything, we really appreciate what you've done for us. And don't worry, once I'm there I'll get him to the hospital, even if I have to drag him there.'

'How are you getting there?'

'I haven't thought about that yet, but I'm sure we'll think of something.'

The sergeant shook my hand, then walked over to Tom and shook his.

'Goodbye Tom, nice meeting you, and if you're ever passing this way again, pop in. Keep in touch guys. I'd love to know how you're doing.'

'We will sergeant' I replied.

The sergeant left the mess and I sat down next to Tom. Looking at him, I could see he looked even thinner than before and his face was gaunt and drawn. I didn't think he'd survive another long trek.

'What's the plan Tom, how are we going to get to Bournemouth? You're in no fit state to walk.'

'You are always worrying Andy, you'll end up with an ulcer if you're not careful.'

Tom took off his hat and gave it to me.

'Rip open the lining, you'll find something in there,' he instructed me.

I couldn't believe it. His hat was full of twenty-pound notes, dozens of them, along with his wallet and a few letters.

'There must be a couple of grand in here!' I exclaimed.

'Keep your noise down, why don't you tell everybody,' said Tom, glancing around suspiciously.

'It's the sergeants mess, not your local pub. You

mean to tell me you've had this money on you all this time, even while you've been sitting for hours begging in the freezing cold and eating out of bins. How long have you had this for? I can't believe you Tom. I don't know whether to laugh or cry.'

'I forgot I had it, honest. I've only just remembered.' He gave me an innocent look.

'Bollocks. Where did you get it all from?'

I sat waiting for an answer but without success. I should have known he wouldn't answer my question, he never did.

'Never mind that, book a taxi, we're going to the seaside,' he replied, his voice full of excitement.

We left the sergeants mess and made our way to the laundry to pick up our clean clothes. Before we put them on, I gave Tom a quick wash down and for once he didn't moan or grumble. Before we left the laundry, I put the tracksuits that we'd been wearing in the washer and started the cycle. Satisfied that we both looked as clean and tidy as we had been when we left Derby, we headed to the guardroom. Angie would be proud of us if she could see us now. After ordering a taxi at the guardroom, we waited inside the barrack gates for it to arrive. It had just started to rain. Tom didn't seem to notice the rain. He had a far away look in his eyes and a smile on his face, as though he was remembering a good time from his past. It wasn't long before I spotted the taxi making its way to the barracks.

'Taxi in the name of Rogers,' the driver called out.

'That's right,' I replied.

We climbed in the back of the taxi and I made sure Tom was comfortable.

'Where to mate?' the driver asked.

'Bournemouth please,' I answered.

'Right, out you get. I'm not in the mood for jokes,' said the driver.

'I'm not joking. We want to go to Bournemouth.'

'Bournemouth is over forty miles away. Unless you've got a hundred and twenty quid, you ain't going anywhere. Looking at the pair of you, I doubt you've got the price of a pint between you.'

I felt like punching him in the face for insulting us, but I counted out a hundred and forty quid and gave it to him. His attitude changed completely.

'Right, Bournemouth it is then!'

We sat back in our seats and waved goodbye to the gateman. Another chapter of my life on the road was about to begin. I glanced back through the rear window and wished I'd never left the army. It was the one time in my life when I was truly happy. Being back in the barracks had made me feel human again and not the invisible man I had become on the streets.

'That was good of them wasn't it Tom, they didn't have to do all that for us did they?'

Tom didn't answer; he was already asleep. He'd only had a few lagers. I think he was just worn out. It had been an emotional day for him what with losing Wolfgang. We'd been travelling for about thirty minutes and I asked the driver how much longer before we arrived in Bournemouth. I was concerned that Tom might want to use the toilet.

'Oh, about another hour, it'll be rush hour soon. We might get held up. Whereabouts do you want dropping off in Bournemouth? I don't know the area that well you see.'

'Anywhere on the seafront will do' I replied.

I was right to be concerned. Tom had wet himself again. I could see the stain spreading across the front of his trousers. I had to think fast. We didn't want to be left on the roadside again.

'Is it alright if we get changed in the back of your cab?'

'You can do what you want, you're paying,' the driver said, shrugging his shoulders.

I woke Tom up from his sleep. 'Tom, wake up mate, we need to get those clothes off you. We can put our tramp clothes back on.'

We got some strange looks from the driver, who was looking through his rear-view mirror.

'Was it worth it?' he asked. 'You look like a couple of extras from an Oliver Twist film.'

Getting changed in the back of the cab was a bit of a struggle, but we managed it. Tom seemed happier now he had his old clothes back on.

'What's this all about guys, going to a party or something?'

'Shall we tell him Tom?'

'It's up to you Andy,' Tom replied, playing along.

I looked down and took a deep breath to stop myself from laughing at the idea that I'd formed in my head.

'Listen driver, if I tell you why we have to dress like this don't say a word to anyone, ok?'

'Ok, your secret is safe with me, and my name's Ken by the way.'

'Right Ken... We are undercover Special Forces and we're about to go on a mission, and the mission is, to mix with the rough sleepers, tramps and the homeless people of Bournemouth.'

'You're winding me up,' replied the driver.

'We have been deployed by the government onto the streets, to sniff out returning ISIS fighters, who are arriving in boats from their crumbling caliphate in Syria and Iraq and are now trying to hide amongst the great unwashed of Bournemouth. So now you are part of the operation,' I said.

I could tell by the look on his face that he believed every word I had uttered. His next comment confirmed it.

'I get it now... that's why I had to pick you up from inside the barracks and the change of clothes, that's why you want to go to the sea front. It all makes sense now.'

'Can I ask you a favour Ken, can you keep a look out and make sure we're not followed?'

'Ok, I'll keep a sharp eye out.'

I sat back and looked over at Tom, who was trying his best to keep a straight face. For the rest of the journey, our new Co Agent Ken was too busy looking out for terrorists, to bother with us. Tom could crap himself all he wanted. This guy would never kick us out now.

'I bet it's nice to get that old onion back on, eh Tom,' I said.

Tom was busy searching his pockets. He looked worried.

'Looking for something?' I asked.

'Yes...my hat. I can't find my hat.'

'I've got it Tom.' I took it out the bag and placed it on his head.

While searching for his hat, he had pulled out an old packet of dog biscuits. Tom looked confused and then anxious.

'Andy we've got to go back, we forgot Wolfgang.'

'Wolfgang is with Angie, Tom. She's looking after him, remember?' I said, knowing he'd already forgotten what had happened earlier today.

'Yes, I forgot, she's a good woman you know, that Angie. Andy, I need to tell you something.'

Tom looked so frail. I decided once we'd visited the beach, I'd get him to the hospital as quickly as possible.

'What is it buddy, what do you want to tell me?'

'They told me to stop drinking a year ago you know. They said if I didn't stop I'd be dead within six months. I think I'm dying Andy.'

So, all the time we'd been together, I'd been watching him kill himself. I even stole the booze for him.

'Don't talk like that Tom; you're not dying mate. They told you six months and you're still here. So, what does that tell you? It tells you they were wrong. I'll tell you what we'll do, when we've been on the beach, we'll get you to the hospital' I said, expecting him to argue against going.

'Ok Andy, you win this time, after the beach though.'

It sounded like Tom had given up. There was no more stubbornness. I put my arm around him and gave him a hug. I felt protective towards him, even more so after his confession.

'Don't worry Tom, we'll get through this, you'll see.'

We were now about ten minutes from Bournemouth and Ken opened his partition window.

'Nearly here gents,' he said 'bloody hell, those tramp suits are realistic aren't they? You even smell like tramps so you'll have no problem fitting in.'

We stopped on the sea front. I gave Ken an extra tenner tip. Tom stood beside me, staring out to sea.

'Thanks, and remember, not a word, right Ken.'
'Good luck with the mission. I hope you get them all.'

Ken drove away still thinking we were Special Forces. What's the betting that he'll be dining out on that story for years to come? He'd left us standing outside an arcade, close to the pier, where there was one of those old fashioned, laughing clown machines. Ironically, here we were, dressed as tramps, surrounded by holidaymakers, who gave us a wide berth, smiling and staring, while the clown laughed and laughed and it felt like it was at us. Tom didn't have a clue what was going on. We purchased two ice creams and headed for the beach and Tom shuffled along behind me. We tried to get well away from people, so we could sit in peace. We found a clear spot, about fifteen metres from the water's edge. There were only a few people near us including a young boy and his father, who were trying to fly a kite, and a young couple holding hands, waist deep in the water, trying to buck up enough courage to go to the next level.

'Well Tom, we made it.'

Tom just sat there and scanned the horizon. He looked contented and happy; he was smiling. I detected a single tear travelling down his face, but it could have been caused by the wind.

'Eat your ice cream Tom, it's melting.'
'My dad always promised me he'd take me to the

seaside. He never did you know. Isn't it wonderful Andy?'

Tom was like a little kid; his face was full of wonder and excitement. He looked like he'd reached the Holy Grail. We sat silently for a while and all we could hear was the refreshing sound of the breaking waves. I really did believe him now, about him never having been to the seaside.

'We've come this far, shall we nick a boat Tom, and paddle over to France. What do the French tramps drink? Is there an extra strong version of their lager do you reckon?'

Tom started to point out at sea. He was like a child on Christmas morning.

'Look, I can see a ship. I wonder where it's going? To some far off place I suppose. I wish I was on that ship, sailing away over the horizon…free as a bird.'

'Where would you go Tom?' I asked, looking at the ship that Tom had spotted.

He didn't answer me.

'Where would you go? It's a big world out there, you know.'

He still didn't answer me. I looked over, just as his ice cream fell out of his hand onto the sand. He slumped forward.

'Are you, ok mate?'

I leaned over to support him. He was struggling to breathe, so I shouted out for help. People started to gather round. Someone used a mobile to call for an ambulance.

'Don't leave me Andy. Promise you won't leave me,' he begged.

'I won't leave you buddy. I'm not going anywhere.'

His last words before he lost consciousness were. 'I'm scared Andy.'

CHAPTER 13

The ambulance arrived and it wasn't long before we were in A&E. The paramedics, as expected, asked me all sorts of medical questions, assuming I was family or something. I couldn't answer them. I didn't know his medical history; nobody knew his medical history. I felt useless. The only information I could give them was that he was admitted to Royal Derby Hospital in March, and his name was **Thomas Rogers**.

The hospital was busy, it was a hot day and Bournemouth was full of holidaymakers. After a long wait, Tom was placed in one of the bays and I stayed with him. It was a while before a doctor arrived to assess him. Tom was still unconscious. He checked him over; at the same time he began asking me more questions. I gave him as much information as I could about how he'd been acting during the short time I'd known him.

'Didn't you find his medical records? I gave the paramedic his name,' I said.

'I'm sorry we couldn't find any details for him, I'm afraid. Without his date of birth it's an impossible task, there are more than one Thomas Rogers listed.'

'You need to phone Royal Derby A&E and ask them

if they know of Tom the tramp. They'll know all about Tom, I'm sure.'

'Listen, why don't you go and get a coffee, while we carry out further tests.'

'He asked me not to leave him on his own.'

'If he wakes up, we'll call for you, what's your name?'

'Andy, my name's Andy.'

'Are you related?'

'No, just a friend, we're both homeless. I mean tramps. I'm his only friend.'

Then I remembered the photograph of the young girl, inside his wallet.

'Hold on, I think he might have a relative. I have a number in my pocket.'

'Well, I suggest you call it. Tom is very, very, poorly,' the doctor said.

The doctor arranged for me to make the call on one of the hospital phones. I sat down and rang the number. It started to ring. I didn't expect an answer so quickly.

'Hello... hello who's there?' the female voice at the end of the phone asked.

I was lost for words. I hadn't had time to think what to say.

'Hello,' the voice said again.

At first the words just wouldn't come out. 'Hi, where do I start... err... I'm a friend of Tom's.'

'Tom, my brother Tom?' the voice was full of concern.

'Yes.'

'What's happened? My name's Maria, I'm his sister.'

'He's in a bad way. He's ill in hospital. I found your

number in his wallet, on the back of a photograph.'

She sounded upset. 'Where are you?'

'In the hospital.'
'Which hospital?'
'Bournemouth.'

There was a short pause before she replied.

'I had a feeling you were going to say that, how bad is he?'

'He's a very poorly man, I'll put the nurse on, and she'll tell you what's happening.'

'What's your name?'
'My name's Andy.'

'Listen Andy, as soon as I've spoken to the nurse, I'll head straight there, thanks for calling.'

I passed the phone to the nurse, and then I went to grab a coffee in the canteen and sat down for a while. By the time I got back to the bay, Tom had been moved. They'd taken him to the isolation ward. They told me I wouldn't be allowed to see him for a while. So, I headed back to the canteen and waited for the next few hours. I had told the nurse where I was going and that I was waiting for Tom's sister. I thought every female that walked into the canteen was Tom's sister, until I'd checked the photo. After another three cups of coffee, there she was. She didn't look much different to the picture, just slightly older. I didn't need the picture to know that it was her, she was the spitting image of Tom, only a younger, prettier version. I was glad I'd taken the time to change back into the clothes that Angie had picked out at the charity shop, or God knows what she would have thought of me. I walked up to her and introduced myself.

'Hi, I'm Andy, I take it you're Maria?' I said by way of introduction.

'Hi Andy, nice to meet you.'

I felt at home with her straight away, she seemed very friendly.

'Sit down, let me get you a coffee,' I offered.

'No, it's ok, I'll get them,' she replied, heading to the counter.

That had been a bit of a gamble because I didn't have any money left anyway. I didn't want to spend any more of Tom's, it didn't feel right. She arrived back at the table with two coffees. She sat down opposite me and smiled.

'We can't see Tom until he's been in for tests they said,' I informed her.

'Yes, I know, they've just told me too.'

Over the next few hours and several more cups of coffee, I told her everything. She was really grateful to me for being there for him, it really showed in her reaction.

'So, you have nowhere to go. You're homeless?'

'Yes' I said. I handed her Tom's hat with all its contents, her photo, his wallet, money and unopened mail.

She looked sad as she inspected each thing. She placed her hand over her mouth and started to cry.

'The stubborn, silly fool, why didn't he open the letters?' she asked, as tears made their way down her face.

I felt sorry for her, I wanted to hold her hand to comfort her but I wasn't sure how she'd react. A nurse who told us we could see him soon approached us, but only after we'd seen the specialist. We were taken to a side room. The specialist was already there; we both knew he was about to deliver bad news. This time I did hold her hand.

'I'm sorry to have to tell you. Tom has multi organ failure due to his many years of alcohol abuse, and the wear and tear of walking the streets. I'm afraid Tom is dying' the specialist said.

'Isn't there anything you can do?' Maria asked.

'I'm really sorry, no. The only thing we can do for Tom now, is to make him as comfortable as possible.'

'I kept telling him to see a doctor,' I said, shaking my head, not wanting to believe what I was hearing.

'Don't blame yourself; looking at his records from Royal Derby Hospital, Tom discharged himself from hospital on three occasions. Tom knew he was dying a while ago.'

'So, the shuffling, the memory loss and the double incontinence, are all related?' I asked.

'Yes, the long term effects of alcohol are capable of damaging nearly every organ and system in the body.'

'Can we go and see him now, is he awake, will he recognise us?' I wanted to see my friend; I'd made him a promise.

'Certainly. Of course you can. He is awake and in good spirits. He's just very tired. I'm sorry I've had to give you the bad news. The nurse will take you to his room.'

Maria sat crying silent tears. The news had torn me apart emotionally, it must have been worse for her.

'Can you just give us a moment?' I said to the nurse.

The nurse and the specialist left the room. It all felt really strange, me sitting here in a room, comforting a woman that I'd only just met.

'I'll be ok,' she said. It's all come as a shock. I never knew he was poorly, I didn't even know he had a drink problem.'

'Are you ok to go and see him now?'

'Yes, of course,' she replied, squaring her shoulders and dabbing her eyes with a tissue.

We stood up, left the room and followed the nurse down the corridor. Tom had his own room, he lay there asleep, he didn't look in any pain, and there were tubes and wires everywhere. It upset me to see him in such a bad way.

'Tom, it's me Andy, I've bought someone to see you,' I said, drawing close to his bed.

Tom opened his eyes. The smile on his face said it all. He looked so happy to see his sister and he held out his hand. Maria reached out to him and sat down. I decided to leave them alone for a few minutes, while I chatted to the nurse outside. Looking through the narrow glass panel in the door, I could see Maria hugging Tom. After about five minutes, I went back in the room. I sat opposite Maria and held Tom's hand. It wasn't long before a young Asian doctor entered the room. He had been given the task of telling Tom the bad news about his condition. In other words, to tell Tom gently that he was dying. I felt sorry for the doctor being given the task, it somehow didn't 'seem fair. Tom took it pretty well; after all, it was something he knew already.

'Well, Tom,' said the doctor 'Is there anything you didn't understand or anything you want to ask me?'

Tom took a while to answer him, then took the young doctor's wrist and said with a smile, 'I haven't got a clue which one to choose, the Co-op or Hurry's.'

The young doctor looked confused. Maria and me started to laugh, we were both used to his dark sense of humour. In other words, he was asking the doctor which undertaker he thought was the best or the cheapest. We both sat with Tom for most of the evening. He hardly spoke, but he knew we were there because he occasionally opened his eyes and smiled. At 01.22 hours Tom passed away in his sleep, it was quick. He wasn't in any pain. Maria kindly gave me the money to stay at a guesthouse that night, and the next day she arranged for Tom's body to be transferred to Burnt Oak in London, the place where he was bought up.

We sat in a pub on the sea front talking about Tom, and I told her all the adventures we had got up to together. She loved the pavilion story and his dog Wolfgang. She was concerned when I told her the reason we had to leave Derby in a hurry. I also told her how I became homeless. I hoped she would tell me more about Tom, but she seemed more interested in hearing about his life on the streets.

'The poor bugger, it's a wonder he kept going with all those things wrong with him' I said, thinking about my old friend.

'He was probably holding on to the only time in his life when he felt wanted' Maria said 'and that's thanks to you. That, and he finally got to do what he always wanted to do, sit on the beach at Bournemouth. So, what will you do now, Andy?'

'Head back up to Derby I suppose. I just hope the people who were targeting me, have moved on to someone else.'

'Will you stay on the streets?'

'No, to be honest with you, the only reason I stayed on the streets at the end, was Tom. I needed him, and he needed me. If it wasn't for him, I don't know what would have happened to me. He always told me that I needed to get myself sorted out and off the streets and I'd reply by saying you need to see a doctor. I suppose we were both as bad as each other.'

We'd been chatting away for a few hours. It was all one way. She wanted to know all about her brother's last days. She cried a few times, sometimes with laughter, sometimes with sadness, especially when I told her how Wolfgang died.

'Well, if you're heading up to Derby, how will you get there? I could give you a lift, I don't mind,' she said.

'Don't be silly, that's a long way, and you've been awake most of the night.'

'How will you get there then?' she asked in a stern, but friendly voice.

'I'll be ok, I got down here, didn't I?'

Maria then reached into her bag and handed me Tom's old hat.

'I want you to have this. It will be something to remind you of Tom.'

'Are you sure, thank you.'

Looking at his treasured hat brought tears to my eyes. Tom had never been without it during the short time I'd known him. On closer inspection, I realised it was full of Tom's money.

'I'm sorry, I'll take the hat, but I don't want the money.' I took the money out and pushed it across the table towards her. She pushed it back to me.

'I insist, there's enough money in there to get you back up to Derby, and back on your feet, for now anyway. I want you to have it. Tom, would have wanted you to have it.'

'Maria, it doesn't matter how many times you tell me. I won't take it, put it back in your bag please.'

'You know, you sound just like Tom, no wonder you got on so well. There is another alternative to returning to Derby. Why don't you come back with me? You can stay at my house until you get back on your feet.'

I felt slightly awkward. The thought of having a roof over my head again urged me to say yes, but I couldn't do it. It just didn't seem right.

'No, you're ok, I couldn't possibly do that, and you don't even know me.'

'I think I do, please say yes, you could stay until you get yourself sorted.' before I could reply, Maria stood up and said 'I've made my mind up. You're coming with me, and anyway, I don't want to be the only one at my brother's funeral.'

How could I say no. I didn't want to miss Tom's funeral and I knew if I returned to Derby, then I probably would.

'Ok, so you're willing to take in a complete, stranger?' I asked, giving her the opportunity to change her mind.

'Yes, Andy, I am.' She was just as stubborn as her brother had been.

Half an hour later we were in the car on our way to London. I spent the first part of the journey listening to Maria's story. She worked on the London underground, but was studying to be a drama teacher. Judging by Tom's acting skills in the shop, and the begging routine with the limping Wolfgang, it must run in the family. She went on to tell me that she'd never married; she'd never had time for all that. At that stage I must have fallen asleep. I hadn't slept properly since the night in the field on Salisbury Plains.

'Andy, Andy, wake up we're nearly there. You fell asleep,' she said, as I opened my eyes.

'I'm sorry. I didn't mean to.'

'Yes, you did. I was boring the pants off you wasn't I?' she replied with a smile.

Now I wonder where she got her wit? She was most definitely Tom's sister.

'You really got on with my brother, didn't you? Did he ever tell you he was my twin?' she asked.

Was I awake, did I hear her right? I thought she was joking. There was no way they could be twins Tom must have been at least twenty years older than her.

'I doubt that, his baby sister more like,' I said.

'No, Tom was my twin brother,' she insisted.

'There's no way you're that old.'

'Oh, thank you very much. How old do you think I am then?'

'Well, Tom never said, but I reckon he was in his late fifties and at a guess I'd say you're in your thirties.'

Maria went quiet for a time. I saw a stray tear roll down her cheek.

'I'm sorry, have I upset you?' I asked.

'No, you haven't upset me. I'm thirty-six and so was Tom, in fact, I'm thirty two minutes older than him.'

I was confused now. 'How could that be? It doesn't make sense. Tom was in the army during the seventies, I saw his ID card. I'm sorry but I don't believe you Maria.'

'Did Tom tell you he was in the army?' she asked, as she concentrated on the road ahead.

'You're joking; it was like getting blood from a stone. He knew all about the army, but I could never get him to talk about his military career.'

'Tom hit the streets when he was seventeen, almost twenty years ago,' she said.

I shook my head. I was finding it hard to believe what she had said. I think she realized I was struggling to accept what she was saying.

'I need to show you something,' she said.

She didn't speak again. She just drove. A while later we stood in her local cemetery looking down at a gravestone.

Here lies the body of Thomas Edward Rogers

16 AUGUST 1958 - 8 JUNE 1990

'This is our father. He served in the army for fourteen years; he did two tours of Northern Ireland and served in Germany and Belize. My mum died a few months after he left in 1988, she died of breast cancer.' Tears streamed unchecked down her face as she spoke.

'That explains a lot. That's the reason he knew so much about the military. It all makes sense now' I said, still finding it hard to believe that Tom had been almost the same age as me.

'He was an amazing dad and Tom adored him, he was always by dad's side. We were both ten when he died,' Maria continued.

'How did your dad die, what happened?'

'My dad started drinking after my mum died, it was if his whole world had fallen in on him, but he always put on a brave face for us. He said to us every year "I'll take you to the seaside this summer, Bournemouth, because that's where I met your mum. We'll sit on the beach and eat an ice cream, you'll see." But we never did. We could never afford it. My dad started to drink so much that we ended up being put into foster homes. We hated being in foster care. Tom and me were separated for a time and we didn't see each other for a whole year. One day, this man came and told us our dad had died. He died of alcoholic poisoning. Tom took it really badly. He could never get over it. After he left school at sixteen he wanted to join the army, but he had a criminal record for a few minor offences and was told he had to wait for two years. He got a job for a while as an apprentice tailor. Then he got in with a bad crowd and started taking drugs. He got involved in petty crime, shoplifting, fighting and eventually he lost his job. That's how he ended up on the streets. It didn't matter what I said to him, he said he was happy on the streets and he didn't want any other life. The house I live in belongs to both of us. Dad left it to the two of us in his will, but Tom didn't want a penny, he just wasn't interested. He wanted to be free…'

'Free as a bird,' I said.

'How did you know I was going to say that?' asked Maria.

'He was a good man, your brother. It's the life he chose and he lived it to the max, it's just a shame that time caught up with him.'

We looked down at their father's grave. My thoughts turned to Tom's reaction to the seaside. I was glad he'd achieved his wish to visit Bournemouth.

'Well, they'll be together now, eh, sitting on the beach no doubt, sharing an ice cream.'

'Or a can of lager,' Maria added. We both laughed.

The funeral took place two weeks later. We weren't the only people to turn up. When word got out around the area, that Tom had passed away, he was more popular than ever. Over a hundred people turned up for the funeral, including Angie, who had delayed her holiday. She came down, bringing Yogi and some other of Tom's homeless buddies. We even received a wreath from the sergeant's mess at Battlesbury Barracks. I'd written to them, thanking them for looking after us and informing them of Tom's death. I made sure he was buried in his coat and hat. I knew he would have wanted that, both items had been a part of who he was.

The food and drink at Tom's wake was all free. There was no pinching pints or mine sweeping the leftovers. We even let Yogi sing, he was awful, but no one told him that!

'Tramps all over Britain will be flying their trousers at half mast today, in remembrance.' I told Maria. She just smiled.

Before Angie left, to head back up to Derby, with her car full of sleeping tramps, she took me to one side.

'When you and Tom escaped from Derby, the public started an appeal, to get you both off the streets. The public love a hero. So, this is the amount that they raised,' Angie said. She handed me a cheque for over sixteen thousand quid!

'But I hardly did anything,' I replied, pushing it back into her hands.

'Take it, it's yours, and don't be a stranger, come up and see me when you get yourself sorted out.' Angie was determined that I took the cheque.

'I will do Angie,' I replied and I meant it.

I wondered why a strange man was hanging around, taking photographs. He was from Derby's local newspaper, Angie informed me. The readers will want to know that I'd received the money they raised. It felt odd being thought of as a hero, I'd only done what any law-abiding person would do. I posed for a few pictures with Angie and the cheque and asked the photographer not to reveal where I was living, for obvious reasons.

I ended up staying in London. And you've guessed it, Maria and me became more than friends. I started to train as a male nurse and Maria became a drama teacher. As for the money, well, that paid for our wedding a year later. As for the other half of the money, which was Tom's, I donated it to a homeless charity in Derby, in memory of Thomas Rogers junior.

I was the happiest ex tramp in the world.

Clive Ward

STREET LIFE

Walking these lonely streets,
The cold, wet floor beneath your feet,
It becomes your bed most nights,
But where exactly will you sleep tonight?

Doorways filled with defeated souls,
Their home now the streets so cold,
No family or friends to turn to,
Oh the sad and lonely few.

The stench of faeces and sick,
The pungent smell of alcohol where they kip,
Passers-by try not to look,
Thankful that they are not stuck in the same ruck.

Tattered and stained clothes,
No washing for these nomads in their temporary abode,
Every cigarette and every penny a prize,
Every day the same each morning they arise.

While some may grab a bite to eat,
Others feed on a liquid treat,
Drugs and violence are commonplace here,
There is no comfort on these streets... Only fear.

They stagger out of the pubs,
They roll out from the clubs,
They are all a threat,
Let's beat up that tramp for a laugh or a bet.

You can be any age rich or poor,
A veteran who's returned home from the ravages of war,
You can be black or you can be white,
At any time and for anyone, homelessness can strike.

We know not of their past,
How life can change too fast,
We must not walk by and simply judge,
Without asking 'what if that was us?'

James Cooper 2018

GLOSSARY

Army dogs - socks

Bergen- backpack

Cam nets- camouflage nets for vehicles and large objects

Compo- ration packs given to troops in the field

Delhi belly- upset stomach

Doss/gonk bag- sleeping bag

Dump- defecation

Endex- end of exercise

Guard mount- inspection of troops before guard duty

IMBER- is an uninhabited village. The entire population was evicted in 1943 to provide an exercise area for American troops preparing for the invasion of Europe, during the Second World War. After the war the resident were not allowed back into the homes. It remains to this day under the control of the MOD and is used for urban warfare training.

Intel brief- intelligence briefing

Man down- incapacitated

Minging- disgusting

M.O- medical officer

RBL- Royal British Legion

RSM- Regimental Sergeant Major

Sofa surfing- sleeping on friends' sofas

Stag- on duty

Stick man- Best turned out soldier on guard duty

Tab- marching

Trap doors- toilets

Clive Ward

Homeless Free as A Bird

Homeless Free as A Bird